TAKING THE HANDOFF

LA WOLVES · BOOK FOUR

CADENCE KEYS

 Created with Vellum

For all those who were the weird kid when they were little. This one's for you.

ONE

Emma

"No."

"Drew..."

"No, absolutely not."

I stare at my brother while he looks around my brand-new apartment in the MacArthur Park neighborhood of Los Angeles. When I researched places to live within my budget a month ago, I stumbled on this modern apartment complex painted a ceramic red. The pictures showed a clean, albeit small studio right near the park. I fell in love with the idea of living here, and after a couple of other searches, I decided to rent out this apartment before someone else snatched it up. It was an exciting new prospect.

Unfortunately, I can understand my overprotective older brother's dismay, because the room we're standing in looks nothing like the pictures online. The walls are stained, the floors are dirty, and the building itself has a vibe that makes you question whether it's safe or not.

But I've come this far. I'm not giving up on my dream now, and this apartment is the first step in making my music dreams come true.

"It's not that bad…"

Drew throws me a *get real* look, and I turn back to the room before us.

Okay, it is that bad, but at least the neighborhood looks decent, even if the few people we've seen seem a little standoffish. But I'm used to that. I come from Seattle, where out-of-towners have aptly named our friendliness the Seattle Freeze because we're so cold to people we don't know. It's sad, but true.

You know what? It's fine. This is just a small hiccup. It doesn't change my plans, and hopefully I won't have to live here long, but I *do* have to live here because it's all I can afford. My parents refused to help because they think I'm chasing after a silly dream that will never make me a living. Truth is, I don't want their money. I don't want their judgment to taint this experience for me. I know they'll never approve of my dreams, so it's more important to me than ever that I do all this on my own.

I was desperate to get out of Seattle and away from my overbearing parents. They might not be so judgy if I was a lawyer like my brother or using my expensive business degree the way it was intended, but I'm not. I'm a singer. It's the only thing I've ever really loved to do. I went to college and got a degree in business, but I felt like I was dying the entire time.

Maybe that's dramatic, but it's the truth.

I have no idea where my creative gene came from because my parents, Mark and Patricia Delaney, don't have a creative bone in their bodies. They're clinical, methodical, and disciplined. It's what makes them such great doctors—my dad an award-winning pediatric surgeon, who discovered a new technique for repairing atrial septal defects in children, and my mom a world-renowned cardiothoracic surgeon. They were thrilled to have a son who thought similarly to them, even if he chose to practice law instead of medicine. Unfortunately, four years after Drew was born, they were gifted with me, their constant disappointment.

I was the weird kid who put on a "circus" performance on the playground jungle gym pretending I was some Cirque du Soleil prodigy. Really, I was just sliding down the sloped parallel bars with my hands out and thinking I looked cool because I switched sides while doing it. I had very few friends and probably would've been plagued by constant bullies if it weren't for Drew and his best friend, Luke Carter.

The thought of Luke awakens butterflies in my stomach that I immediately push aside, opting not to revisit my lifelong crush when there are more important things to worry about.

I look around my studio apartment, and a spark of creativity zings through my veins as I see all the possibilities of this space come to life in my head. It may be small and not nearly as clean as the listing claimed, but it's mine and it's a blank slate ready to be turned into something new and vibrant. A trip to Target and I'll have this place looking new and homey in no time.

The steady beats of a new song start in the back of my mind, and I quickly dig in my purse for the notebook I keep for moments just like this. I jot down the few lines that started repeating in my head moments ago before tucking it back in my purse.

I look up to see Drew staring at me, a small smile on his face.

"Did this hellhole inspire you?"

I roll my eyes at his exaggeration. It's not a hellhole. It's not nice, or as posh as he's used to, but it's mine and I'll make it into my own little oasis. I don't see any signs of rodents, so that's a plus.

"You can't honestly believe I'm going to let you live here, Emma."

"Of course you are because it's not up to you. I'm the one

paying the rent. Don't stress about it, D. It'll be fine. I'll spruce it up, and it'll look cute in no time."

He shakes his head. "You're so determined to make this work that you're willing to live in this shit stain of an apartment?"

"Can you please stop talking about my new home like that? It's got potential. And it's in my budget. It'll be fine."

It has to be fine. I don't have a backup plan, and singing is the only thing that's ever given me true joy and happiness. I moved to Los Angeles to pursue a career, and I'm not going to let my overprotective brother stand in my way, even if a small part of me worries he might be right about this apartment. I know he means well. He's always looked out for me and been my biggest supporter. He always stood up for me to our parents, especially when I didn't have the strength to do it myself, and he pushed me to pursue this crazy dream of mine. He's the closest thing to a best friend I've ever had, and he knows how important this move is to me.

Drew sees my resolve and then shakes his head in disbelief. "I'm gonna step outside. I've got to make a call."

"Who are you calling?"

"Don't worry about it."

"You're not calling Mom and Dad, are you?"

He must hear the hint of worry in my tone because his expression softens, and he shakes his head before coming over and placing his hands on my shoulders. "I'm not calling Mom and Dad. I promise. Don't worry about them. They'll come around someday. Keep following your dreams, Squish. You know I've always got your back when it comes to them, right?"

I nod and fight back the tears I feel burning behind my eyes. I will not cry, even if my brother's words soothe the ever-present worry that I will always be a disappointment to my parents. At least I'll always have Drew.

TWO

Luke

"I may need your help with Emma."

I chuckle softly. "What did she get herself into this time?"

My best friend, Drew Delaney, sighs loudly and says, "Dude, if you saw this apartment, you'd understand. It's in MacArthur Park, and it's a dump. I got a bad vibe about the place."

Why does it not surprise me that little Emma Delaney accidentally rented an apartment in an area of town she has no business being in? Especially not living alone.

Emma has always marched to the beat of her own weird little drum. Her flaming red hair, face overrun with freckles, multi-colored glasses, and the braces she got when she was thirteen all made her stand out—unfortunately not in a good way. She was constantly getting teased, although Drew and I did our best to block the insults from ever reaching her. She got enough shit from her parents; she didn't need it from the kids at school. Kids can be brutal, and they rarely know the lifelong damage their thoughtless insults can cause. Both Drew and I wanted to shield her from that as much as possible.

I've known Drew my whole life. We grew up as neighbors in

an affluent part of Seattle. He's my brother in all the ways that matter and my found family, especially since my own parents have always been too busy rubbing elbows with the rich and powerful for their own selfish gains to really be tender, loving parents. As much as I care about my parents, they only had a kid because it was socially expected. Drew was my saving grace during their tumultuous marriage and their bitter, nasty divorce. He's my ride or die and the one person who knows me better than anyone else.

Unlike Emma, bullying wasn't something Drew and I ever had to contend with. We were both popular jocks. Drew in basketball, me in football. Since Drew was practically my family, I didn't hesitate for a second when he asked me to help him guard his little sister from the nasty insults floating around about her. But we could only do so much since we were four years older than she was. Drew told me more than once how worried he was for her in high school. Not only did she have to deal with mean, punk-ass rich kids, but she also had to go home to two parents who nitpicked her constantly.

It's been five years since I last saw Emma. She was studying abroad the last time I was home for any length of time. And since the blowout fight with my dad, I haven't been back unless it was to play the Seahawks. Drew comes down to LA a couple of times a year when it works with my schedule, and we also take a yearly boys' trip somewhere and catch up on whatever we've missed through phone calls and texts.

"So, what do you need from me?" I ask him.

His voice gets quiet like he doesn't want to be overheard. "I'm not sure yet. You know how stubborn Emma can be. I can't tell her what to do, or she'll stay put just to prove me wrong. But she can't stay here. I'd love to have a backup plan ready for her if this goes south."

"Yeah, that's probably a good idea."

"Do you think if she agrees, she could stay with you just until she finds another place and gets her feet under her here in LA?"

My back stiffens. I haven't had a roommate since Drew and I lived together during our four years at the University of Washington. I'm not exactly eager to have someone else in the one place that has become my sanctuary. I like my private time away from the spotlight to reset from the crazy life I sometimes live. But this is Drew. I would do anything for him, just like he'd do anything for me. I know he wouldn't ask if it wasn't important, so despite my hesitation, I reply, "Yeah, as long as it's just temporary."

"It definitely would be. Emma's not going to like relying on you for a place to stay for long. Plus, she already has a waitressing job lined up, so it's just a matter of finding a different apartment that fits within her budget."

"Okay, then yeah. Just give me a call if she decides the apartment won't work out."

"I will. You're the best, man."

"Don't you forget it," I say with a laugh. "Hey, since you're in town, you wanna grab some dinner before you head back to Seattle?"

"That'd be great. Let me get Emma settled in her place. Maybe you can distract me from the fact I'm leaving my sister in this dump."

We agree on a time and place and say goodbye.

"You're shitting me."

I shake my head, stifling a laugh as I sip my beer. "Nope. Although I wish I was. She was hot. I really wish she had passed the gold-digger test."

Drew shakes his head in disbelief. "I can't believe she did that. I mean, I know it was a lie you told her to test her, but to go to the press claiming you have a secret baby with your high school science teacher is insane. How could she honestly think that was true?"

"I was very convincing."

He leans forward, his elbows resting on the edge of the table. "Does it ever get exhausting not knowing who to trust? I mean, when you first got drafted, I thought you had it made. You had these smoke shows tripping over themselves to get in your bed, but not a single one has turned out to be legit."

I shrug. "I think it just comes with the territory."

"But don't you miss having a real relationship? When's the last time you even trusted a woman enough to invite her to your house?"

"It's been a long time."

Don't get me wrong, I love my life. I have a kick-ass house in Los Angeles. I'm a running back for the greatest football team in the NFL, and I get to make a living playing a game I love every day. It's a great life. And truthfully, I haven't believed in love in a long time, so not having a real relationship hasn't bothered me the way I know it would bother Drew.

The first time I questioned if love was real was when I was a kid and found out my dad was a serial cheater and the main reason behind my mom's unhealthy gin consumption. My parents used to spout how much they loved each other in front of their similarly miserable friends, but behind closed doors it was all cutting remarks and screaming matches that left me wishing they'd just get a divorce already. I got my wish when my dad put his dick in my mom's best friend, and they became the scandal of our country club. My mom had been able to brush aside the waitresses on business trips and the nannies that she could let go for other reasons, but she couldn't brush it under the rug when it was such a public offense within their own social circle.

So, she divorced him and then married her divorce attorney, whose wealth almost rivaled my dad's. She got to keep the cushy life she was accustomed to and save face in front of her socialite friends. I thought that would make things easier, but instead my parents found ways to tear each other down through me. I became a pawn in their games against each other and quickly realized love wasn't real. You don't treat someone you love that way, whether it's your spouse or your kid. That's not love. I'm not sure what love is, but it sure as shit isn't that.

If it weren't for Drew, I'm not even sure I'd understand loyalty, but whenever things got extra shitty with my parents, I'd go to his house, and he'd let me vent or rage or just distract me with video games. He's been my saving grace in more ways than one. I owe him more than I could ever repay. Who knows what kind of asshole I would've turned into if I didn't have his friendship to keep me sane and grounded.

Knowing where my mind has wandered off to, Drew asks, "Is your mom still hassling you about talking to your dad?"

My thumbs brush aside the condensation on the glass. "Yeah."

"Are you ever going to tell her the truth about what happened, so she'll lay off?"

"No."

And that's the other reason I stopped believing in love. Four years ago, I was sure I'd met the woman I was going to marry. Anna was bright and bubbly. She got along with the other wives and girlfriends of my teammates. She loved being at home just as much as she loved going out and celebrating with me and the guys. I was ready to propose, which was one of the reasons I brought her home to Seattle for Christmas. My dad was throwing a huge party at his mansion on Lake Washington like he usually does. Everyone from his country club and his office was there. Drew was even there with his parents.

At some point, Anna excused herself to use the restroom. I stayed and chatted with Drew until the caterer asked me if I knew where my dad was. His house is huge, but I knew if he wasn't in the main room with all his guests, there were only about two or three other places he was likely to be. With the caterer on my heels, we went in search of my father. The first room turned up empty. The second room had a guest from my dad's office on his cell phone. I moved to the last location thinking *third time's a charm*, and when I opened the door, I not only found my dad, with his pants around his ankles, but I found Anna on her knees with his dick in her mouth.

I can still remember how quickly bile rose in my throat and how much hate I had for him in that moment—hate that still hasn't receded. How big of a scumbag do you need to be to hook up with your son's girlfriend?

But I guess it all worked out in the end. Anna got to be on the arm of one of the richest guys in Seattle making all the connections she was hoping for—something I'd been blind to when we were together—until she found out he was cheating on her. No surprise. And I created the gold-digger test, which has insured that I never end up with a woman like her ever again.

Changing the topic back to our original conversation, Drew asks, "So, you just gonna stick with one-night stands?"

I heave a sigh. "Fuck, man, those got old a while ago, but I just keep getting burned by these women who are only using me so they can say they dated a pro athlete and maybe have fifteen minutes of fame. It's kind of exhausting. Maybe I should take a break altogether."

Drew stares at me like I just spoke another language and forgot to translate. "Wait. Are you trying to tell me you're not going to get laid at all? Ha! Okay, we'll see how long that lasts."

"What's that supposed to mean?"

He sets his beer back down on the table, and I can totally picture him in the courtroom getting ready to question a witness when he already knows the answers. "I very clearly recall the last time you went on a *break*," he says with air quotes. "You lasted two months before you became a raging asshole from not getting laid. You get whatever the sex equivalent is of hangry. If you don't get it regularly, you become a straight-up grump."

"I do not."

"Do too."

"Do not."

"Okay, what are we, five?"

I roll my eyes at him. "Whatever."

Drew smirks at me like he's already won his case. "Uh-huh. You know I'm right. Just admit it."

Fortunately, I'm saved by the waitress delivering our food. Thank fuck, because I really did not want to admit that he's kind of right. I do get more irritable when I don't get laid regularly, but it also makes me a little sick to admit that. It makes me feel a little too much like my dad, and that's something I swore I'd never be.

THREE

Emma

The bustling restaurant does little to help me stay awake. Three days in my apartment and I've hardly been able to sleep at all. I thought the place looked slightly questionable during that first day with Drew, but that's nothing compared to how the apartment complex transforms to massively sketchy at night.

The first night, someone shook the handle on my front door so forcefully I was convinced they were going to break it right off. My heart was pounding like it was going to burst out of my chest. For a split second, I thought about calling Drew, but I wasn't ready to admit defeat. When I woke up after a fitful night's sleep and saw everything was fine and my apartment was secure, I convinced myself I'd overreacted.

The second night, I heard screaming from my neighbor's apartment. And not the kind of screaming that comes from otherworldly pleasure, but the kind when someone is getting murdered. I stayed awake the rest of the night, my ears perking at every sound, no matter how small. My heart raced every time a noise penetrated the thin, stained walls of my apartment. By the time I made it to my first shift at Walker's Bistro and Brew yesterday, I felt like the walking dead.

When I got home last night, I thought I'd be too tired to do anything but sleep. Joke was on me, though, because not only did I deal with a car continuing to backfire—I refuse to believe it was gunshots—but there was more rattling of my front door handle and even some knocking and whispered words.

Walking into my shift this morning, my eyes feel like sand, and my body already aches from lack of sleep and stress.

"Girl, you look like shit."

The words register in slo-mo, and I dazedly turn my head toward the voice. My eyes land on scuffed black motorcycle boots, up tall, toned legs, over an old Ramones T-shirt, and then pass over the smooth olive complexion and stick-straight black hair of my co-worker. My green gaze connects with Bernie's gray hues. Bernie, short for Bernice, also works at Walker's and took me under her wing on my shift yesterday. Despite my sleep deprivation, she and I bonded instantly. Her own quirkiness made me immediately recognize a kindred spirit.

"Thanks, Bernie," I say sarcastically. Well, I attempt sarcasm, but in my tired state it comes out more slurred and drained.

"Hey, hun, I call it like I see it. What's going on?" Her brow furrows in concern, and tears burn my eyes. I'm so tired. And when I'm tired, I get extra emotional. Which isn't great, because I'm already a pretty emotional person, so I really don't need any help in that department.

At the slide of the first escaped tear down my cheek, I take a shuddering breath, my bottom lip quivering. Bernie's eyes go wide. "Oh shit, I set you off. You better not cry, girl, cause I'm a sympathetic crier, and my eyeliner is on point today."

Another tear slips out, and I let out a quiet sob combined with a laugh as Bernie's comment makes me realize I forgot to even put on makeup today. Bernie frowns, and she quickly looks around before shuffling me through the back of the restaurant and into a room that looks like an office. She sits me down in the closest chair and plants her hands on my shoulders.

"Okay, tell me what's wrong."

"Immmaaaapatahtahat," I wail, the dam breaking and my shoulders shaking from my sobs.

"Hun, I'm gonna need you to speak English."

I huff out a laugh and feel snot pop out of my nose. Lovely. A tissue lands in my fingers, and I bring it up to my nose, wiping the snot away. I suck in a breath, trying to find some composure. My eyelids feel heavier than before, and my chest tightens with fear as I relive the past few nights in my new place.

With each word out of my mouth, Bernie's mouth puckers and concern deepens in her eyes. "Hun, I hate to break it to you, but as cute as parts of that neighborhood are, that is not a place for a single girl to live alone."

Yeah, no shit. I've figured that out already.

"I don't know what to do. I'm afraid to go home."

"I'd let you stay with me, but I have the roommate from hell."

I squint in confusion. "I thought you lived with your boyfriend."

She nods, her face serious. "I do. And he's a fucking slob, so yeah, I don't want you to have to put up with that." She puckers her mouth again. "You said your brother might help?"

My shoulders sag in defeat. I really did not want to have to rely on Drew to help me with this situation even though he offered before he left to go back to Seattle, but I think I'm past that now. I just want out of my place.

Bernie helps me through the rest of my shift, which I would feel bad about if I wasn't so exhausted and didn't desperately need the money from this job. On my way home, I call Drew, conceding.

"Hey, Squish, how's LA?"

"Drew..." My voice breaks before I can get any more out.

"What happened?" he asks, immediately on alert.

I tell him about the past couple of nights.

"Shit, I was worried about this. Would you be willing to go stay with Luke for a few weeks just until you can find a new place in a safer neighborhood?"

My breath catches in my throat.

Luke.

As in Luke Carter. My lifelong crush.

I've been desperately in love with him for as long as I can remember. Of course, he's only ever seen me as Drew's adorkable little sister, but every time he came to my defense in grade school and junior high, I melted. He and Drew made sure no one would mess with me, even though I never quite fit in at our prep school. Luke is the guy I've measured all others against, and no one has ever compared. He's a big reason I didn't date in high school, another being the fact that I had very few friends or guys even interested in me at that point in my life.

I haven't seen Luke in five years, and I've changed a lot in that time. Can I actually *live* with Luke? More importantly, will I be able to hide the feelings he's always brought out?

"Emma? Are you still there?"

Drew's frantic voice pulls me from my thoughts. "Yeah, I'm here."

He lets out a relieved sigh. "Thank God, I was worried someone had snatched you or something. I really want you out of that place. So? Are you okay staying with Luke?"

My heart flutters as the word leaves my throat. "Yeah." Daydreams from the days when I would scribble Emma Carter in my notebooks flit through my mind.

"Where are you now?" my brother asks, pulling me out of my head again.

"On my way home."

"Okay, I'm going to text Luke right now and stay on the phone with you. I want you to pack up as much as you can and then I'll text you the directions to Luke's house. He can come back with you during the day to get the rest of your stuff."

"Okay."

Relief overwhelms me, and not for the first time, I'm incredibly thankful for my brother. My parents would never do this for me. They'd help me come home, but only if I agreed to choose a sensible career.

Once I get to my complex, those pleasant flutters in my heart turn into furious poundings, and my stomach tightens with nervous energy. I grip my phone tight in my hand as I make my way across the parking lot and up the stairs to my apartment, my eyes darting around anxiously the entire time.

I'm just about to reach my door when I notice it's already cracked open. My heart drops to my stomach.

"Drew," I whisper hoarsely into the phone, "my door's already open."

"Get out of there NOW, Emma." He can't hide his panic, which I'm grateful for because it confirms I'm not overreacting about this. Without another thought for my things, I turn on my heel and hightail it back down the stairs. My fingers shake around my key fob, and I'm thankful it opens with the click of a button because there's no way I could get my hands still enough to stick the key in the door.

I slide into my car, my eyes scanning the back seat, terror thrumming steadily through my veins. I quickly shut the door and hit the lock button. A slightly relieved breath releases from my mouth as I feel some semblance of security wrap around me.

Drew texts me Luke's address, and as I put it into the maps app on my phone, a thought hits me like a brick to the chest. "Oh my God, my guitar!"

"Emma, don't even think about it," Drew says sternly, but it barely registers as I think about my most prized possession that I left in its case in my bedroom when I went to work this morning.

"Drew—"

"No, Emma. It's not worth it. If someone was in your apartment, they could still be there."

Tears stream down my face as I glance back out the window toward my apartment. "But—"

"Emma,"—the pain in his voice stops any more words from coming out of my mouth—"you're worth so much more than that damn guitar. I'll buy you a new one. It can be replaced. *You* can't. Please, I'm begging you. Do not go back into that apartment by yourself."

I think those words might be the nicest thing anyone has ever said to me. And hearing the pain in his voice steels my resolve to get out of there, leaving my precious possession behind. I could never do anything to purposefully hurt my brother.

"Okay," I whisper.

I press go on the map's navigation and start my car, heading toward a destination I never expected. The closer I get to Luke's house, the more my stomach tightens with nerves. Will he recognize me? The last time I saw him I was going through a horrible acne phase and hadn't started wearing contacts yet. He still looked at me like he always had—like I was adorable and weird.

But a lot's changed in five years. I studied abroad and traveled extensively, exploring different cultures and mindsets. I found myself in a way I never had before, and my confidence blossomed. Physically, I learned how to actually tame my crazy hair into soft waves, started wearing contacts, and played around with makeup until I found a look that worked for me. I embraced my love of 1950s fashion and started curating a wardrobe that showcased my curves and made me feel sexy as hell.

My brain catalogues all the changes I've made, and with each one, a thrill of possibility fills me and I'm no longer worried about whether Luke will recognize me. By the time I pull up in front of his house only one question blazes through my mind.

Will Luke like what he sees?

FOUR

Luke

Drew's text blazes on my phone screen, and an ominous feeling slides down my spine. I try to call him, but he doesn't pick up which only heightens my unease. When the tentative knock finally comes, I'm already pacing in front of my door, opening it before the person has a chance to let their knuckles fall a second time.

Even though I knew who was coming, the woman standing before me is not what I was expecting at all.

My mouth goes dry as my gaze scours the voluptuous body that is both familiar and completely different from what I remember. Her gorgeous red hair falls in soft waves around her shoulders, stopping just at the edges of breasts that have my dry mouth suddenly watering and desire spreading like wildfire through my veins. I follow the lines of her body wrapped in an outfit reminiscent of a fifties pinup. And fuck, does she have the body to pull it off. My gaze slides back up her curvy frame as my brain tries to make sense that this is the same woman I've known my whole life.

This Emma looks *nothing* like the nerdy, awkward teen I remember. This is a refined, stunningly sexy version of her that has my brain hazy with lust and my dick straining uncomfortably in my jeans.

"Luke?"

Her soft voice holds remnants of fear which shakes me out of my lust fog.

"Emma, what's going on? Are you okay?" Fuck, even my voice sounds hoarse.

"Drew said he texted you?" She says it like a question, probably because I'm standing here staring at her like a fucking psycho.

"Yeah, here, come on in." I step aside and gesture for her to enter. I notice she only has her purse with her. "Drew said you needed to stay with me, but I couldn't get the fucker on the phone to tell me what was going on."

She offers me a small smile. "That's probably because he refused to get off the phone with me until I was here." She holds her phone up, and I can see that a call is still going, and Drew's name is in big bold letters with a goofy picture of him. "He wants to talk to you."

I take the phone from her hand. "Hey, man, what's up?"

"Fucker, huh?" There is a hint of joking in his tone, but it's overshadowed by the worry I can hear there.

"What's going on?"

The more Drew tells me about Emma's apartment and coming home tonight, the more I start to understand his concerns. I glance at Emma, who's biting her lip, her big emerald-green eyes glossy with unshed tears and pink high in her creamy cheeks.

"Can you take her, Luke? I know you said before you would, but I honestly don't know how long it'll take her to get on her feet, and I don't want her in that position again." He takes a heavy breath. "Fuck, man, I was scared out of my mind for her. I can't lose my sister. I don't want her living somewhere dangerous."

"I'll take care of her." I glance at her again and then mentally tell my dick to settle the hell down because Emma is way off-limits. Fuck, she's the goddamn dictionary definition of off-limits. "She can stay with me as long as she needs. We'll find her a new place—that she can afford," I add when I notice Emma shooting a glare my direction. She nods once, and I realize that as hesitant as I was to have her here, I'm relieved I can offer some sense of security for her and Drew.

"Thank you, Luke. You don't know what this means to me."

I focus back on the phone. "Of course I do. You're my ride or die, man. You know I've always got your back, and if that means looking out for Emma, then that's what I'm going to do. She's in good hands, I promise."

I glance back at Emma and have to take a breath at the hooded look in her eyes as she slides them up my body. When her gaze reaches my face, her cheeks flood a bright pink before she drops her gaze to the floor.

But it's too late. I saw the lust in her eyes, and it's already causing my blood to heat and my body to react in a way it never has to her.

Well, not until tonight at least.

My hands itch to touch her, but then Drew's voice comes through the line like a bucket of ice water dumping on my libido.

What the fuck am I doing?

"Sorry, what was that?"

"I was just saying again how thankful I am, and I'm sure Emma is too. That place was sketch as hell." The relief in his voice is evident.

"Like I said, you know I'll always do whatever you need." I turn back to Emma. "Let me let you go, so I can get Em settled."

We say bye, and once I hang up, I pass the phone back to her. She takes it, her graceful fingers grazing against mine for the briefest moment. Her eyes are still downcast.

Her reaction to me isn't all that surprising. Emma's had a crush on me since we were kids—yes, I knew, but I never acknowledged it. What surprises me most is *my* reaction to her. That slight touch has electrified the tip of my fingers and left me reeling from my response to her.

But then reality settles heavily over me, and I remember who she is.

I can't feel anything but familial affection for Drew's sister. Not only would he kill me, but I'd lose his friendship, which would be worse than death. I push aside whatever crazy pull Emma has on me and chalk it up to just my body's way of telling me I need to get laid.

It can't mean anything else.

I'll never do anything to jeopardize my relationship with Drew, and hooking up with his sister would be a huge betrayal of his trust.

My loyalty will always be with Drew.

FIVE

Emma

Damn, Luke got hotter, if that's even possible. He was already every woman's definition of a thirst trap, but now...fuck me, I'm in trouble.

His brown hair looks soft, and my hands twitch at my sides as I think about what it would be like to slide my fingers through it.

The urge is so strong it reminds me of that episode of *Gilmore Girls* where Lane has a crush on her band partner and is dying to slide her fingers through his hair. Then she does it in front of everyone and is completely mortified. I always thought that was so silly. I mean, who just slides their hands through someone's hair like that?

Well, now I know, because I'm on the verge of being that person.

There's nothing more painful than unrequited love. I've spent most of my life either devotedly in love with Luke Carter or cursing his name for making me feel all this love by myself.

I've dated other guys, and even caved and finally gave up my virginity to a guy I dated in London when I was studying abroad. I'd been holding out for Luke—not because I thought my virginity was some special gift or anything, but because I only wanted to be with him—but when he got drafted to the NFL, I knew my chances of ever getting him to notice me were long behind me. He was surrounded by gorgeous models and actresses. Gorgeous *skinny* models and actresses.

I'm not fat, but I'm definitely not skinny. I fall in that awkward middle spectrum, or as one guy I dated called it, thicc. I have a nice hourglass shape that I couldn't find clothes for until I stumbled into a thrift shop my freshman year of college. That's when I discovered that 1950s fashion trends had been made for buxom beauties like me. I decided to embrace my Marilyn Monroe figure, and instead of being the weird girl, I became the eccentric girl who only wears vintage style clothes. Guys started noticing me, and I finally put myself out there, but I had still secretly hoped Luke would notice me and be my first.

Hell, I wanted him to be my forever.

But then I saw him with gorgeous skinny woman after gorgeous skinny woman, and I knew I'd never measure up. With my heart in shambles, I applied to study abroad for a year in London, and that's where I met Simon Asterbury. After he courted me for a month, I gave him the piece of me I'd been saving for someone else.

Simon was wonderful and made it a special experience, but I still cried after he left my place that night because I felt like I'd betrayed my heart. Crazy and ridiculous as it was to feel that way about a man who'd never once seen me as anything but his best friend's little sister, it's how I felt.

While I only dated Simon for a few months, he gave me something I'd never had before—confidence in my body. My parents, my mom in particular, had always been disappointed in my curvier shape. I was constantly encouraged to diet and passive-aggressively fat-shamed by my mom. When you grow up hearing that all the time, it starts to settle deep in your mind that it's the truth.

Finding clothes and a style that enhanced my shape in a positive way was one step to silencing my mom's voice that still lived in my head. Simon was another.

He showed me all the ways he loved my body and my shape and reinforced how beautiful I was not only with words, but with his touch. Where my mom had always poked and pinched at my fat, constantly bringing attention to it, Simon touched me with gentle and tender caresses. He made every inch of my body feel cherished and celebrated. He loved my thick thighs, round ass, and full breasts. Simon boosted my confidence in a way no one else had before, and that confidence continued even after we broke up. It felt like someone had finally turned on the light and allowed me to see who I really was, or could be, for the first time in my life.

I explored my newfound sexuality and blossoming confidence as I traveled across Europe—dancing seductively in nightclubs, wearing outfits I would've never dared to before, and even having a couple of one-night stands.

By the time I returned home, my mom's callous remarks about my plump waist or revealing cleavage rolled right off me. She no longer carried power over me. That realization is what pushed me to finally pursue my dreams instead of following the miserable path my parents had encouraged. I only had one semester left for my business degree and decided it would serve me well to have it in the long run, so I spent my last semester of college putting my plan in place for my move to LA.

I thought I had everything figured out, but I never foresaw the adorable apartment complex in an idyllic little neighborhood was actually in a not so safe part of town. Looking back on it now, I wish I'd had a friend like Bernie who was local and could've warned me.

Then again, if I had, I wouldn't be standing in Luke's house right now.

I let my gaze rove over his fit athletic six-foot, four-inch frame. His brown hair is a little longer on top than I remember, but it's still cut close at the sides. His arms are covered in tattoo sleeves, and my eyes linger on the designs wishing I had more time to study them and figure out if they have any meaning behind them. He had a few tattoos the last time I saw him, but nowhere near this many. I've never been all that drawn to tattoos on other guys, but somehow they fit Luke like they were always meant to be on his body.

Luke turns to me, his hazel gaze connecting with mine and making those butterflies flutter in my stomach the way he always does. My life would be so much easier if I'd met someone else who did that, but it's only ever been Luke.

He frowns slightly, simply staring at me like he doesn't know what to do with me, and I'm quickly reminded that he only sees me as the "little sister" he's had to help Drew look out for most of his life. I shake my head, angry at myself for even thinking I saw a hint of lust in his eyes when he first saw me standing on the other side of his door.

Of course it wasn't lust. My life couldn't possibly be that miraculous.

"Emma?"

"Hmm?" Fuck, did he ask me a question?

"You okay?"

His question reminds me of the whole reason I'm even standing in his living room right now. My nose starts to burn as tears threaten in my eyes, and my heart aches at the idea of my apartment. I feel violated, and the worst part is not knowing if my most prized possession is even still there or already stolen.

The downside of being such an emotional person is I tend to cry at the drop of a hat. Happy? I cry. Sad? I cry. Angry? Yep, I cry.

Right now, I'm feeling all three, so tears fall unbidden down my full cheeks.

Over the years, I've learned to hold them back until I could be alone where no one would be able to see me fall apart, but the events of tonight, in addition to my already exhausted state, have wiped away any control of my emotions I might normally possess.

Worry coats Luke's face. "I know it's been, like, five years since we last saw each other, but I should probably remind you I'm not good with tears."

I observe him, noticing how he's aged so handsomely. He's not the boy I remember, but all man now. His body is strong and fit, likely from his job as a running back for the LA Wolves football team. My gaze slides up his arms to his wide shoulders before finally landing on his ruggedly handsome face, his chin covered with that bit of scruff which always made me weak in the knees—and still does—and his hazel eyes filled with concern and helplessness.

Knowing Luke as well as I do from years of quietly watching him from the sidelines, I know he's about three seconds away from either trying to "handle" the situation and take charge or shut down completely.

The idea that he's this worked up over me makes a laugh explode out of my mouth. His concern instantly morphs to confusion. The expression of helplessness is replaced by a look I'm all too familiar with from other people.

The *what's wrong with the weird girl* look.

Unfortunately, that look on Luke just makes me laugh harder. I bend over, leaning my hands on my thighs while I try to catch a breath. Oh my God, I'm a mess. One minute I'm crying and the next I'm laughing uncontrollably.

When I stand back up, finally able to compose myself, I feel lighter, like all the fear and tension that suffused my body since I first noticed my front door open has finally dispersed. Luke stares at me like he's worried I'm about to grow another head.

"I'm okay, I promise," I attempt to reassure him.

He swallows noticeably, the movement of his Adam's apple catching my gaze. How many times have I thought about licking him right there?

His body shifts, and when I look back at his eyes, his expression is one I've never seen on him before. I could almost convince myself that it's attraction.

My breath stalls in my chest, and the smile falls from my face as we stand there staring at each other. Like it always does whenever I'm around Luke, my body starts to light up at his appraisal. Even if his eyes never leave mine, I feel him everywhere. His gaze probes mine like he's trying to learn every secret I've ever kept hidden. My core tightens, and I feel slickness growing between my thighs, my many fantasies of him coming to life in my head the longer we stand here in our stare-off.

He blinks, breaking the spell, then clears his throat and looks away. I feel the loss instantly, all the warmth spreading through my body gone in a second. I swear I'm going to get whiplash from all the ups and downs of this day.

"I'll show you to the guest room." His voice is gruff and hoarse, and I force myself to focus on reality—he's only doing this for Drew. It's not about me at all.

I follow Luke up the stairs and down his cleanly decorated hallway toward his guest bedroom, reminding myself over and over again that Luke has never seen me as anything other than his best friend's little sister. I try desperately not to let my heart get carried away, but when Luke gives me his handsome smile right before he leaves me in the room, I know it's already too late.

My heart's always been his.

SIX

Luke

I stare at my white ceiling, my thoughts running in circles, all of them encompassing one woman.

Emma fucking Delaney.

Has she always looked like that?

There's no way. I would've noticed.

Would you, though?

She's Drew's sister. Off-limits.

So, why can't I shake this slow burn that's been thrumming through my body since I opened my front door tonight?

I glance at the clock. Okay, technically last night since it's now four in the morning. I'm going to be fucking useless tomorrow. I close my eyes, waiting for sleep to take me, but all I see are Emma's green eyes, her luscious red hair, and those juicy red lips. God, and her fucking curves.

My dick swells as images of my hands caressing those curves flash through my mind. I let out a frustrated groan and pull my pillow over my face.

What the fuck is wrong with me?

Eventually, sleep finds me, but it's fitful and full of dreams of a stunning redhead who I refuse to admit is the woman sleeping in my guest room down the hall. My alarm goes off at eight, and I open my eyes against the bright light streaming through my windows.

Ugh, it's going to be a long-ass day.

I reach for my phone and am immediately greeted by a text from Drew.

Drew: Did Emma get settled all right? I'm worried about her.

I stare for a long time at his words, soaking them in and reminding myself why it's crucial I keep my distance from Emma. Drew can never know that I got a hard-on for his sister. Especially not when he asked me to look out for her. Fantasizing about her and wanting to fuck her is not looking out for her.

His text is just what I need to get my head on straight and focus on what I need to do. I need to put some distance between Emma and me. Keep her at arm's length.

My loyalty is with Drew. I repeat my new mantra in my head at least half a dozen times.

I text him back that she's good and let him know I'm going with her to her apartment today to get the rest of her stuff. She has work tonight, but I'll send a text out to a couple of people I know to see if they have any recommendations on affordable apartments in safe neighborhoods.

Drew trusts me to take care of his sister, and that's what I'm going to do.

My feet step off the last stair, and I immediately spot Emma in the kitchen, her back to me as she waits for the coffee to finish brewing. My gaze, with a mind of its own, wanders across her pert ass wrapped in a tight pair of high-waisted cream pants that stop mid-calf. I quickly avert my gaze, nervous she'll catch me checking her out. She turns just as my gaze moves up, and I freeze for a second, worried she caught me, but she offers me a small smile with no hint that she saw anything.

"Want some coffee?" she asks.

"That would be great, thanks." I walk over and grab a mug from the cupboard while she drops a Keurig cup in the coffeemaker. "How'd you sleep?" I ask.

She shrugs as she drops a spoonful of sugar in her coffee. "Okay, I guess." She glances up at me, her green eyes so expressive I can see every emotion she's feeling flit across her face. "I'm scared to go back there," she says quietly.

"I'll go with you."

She nods, like that's exactly what she expected I'd say.

"I have to be at work at four, so we should probably head over there soon. Let me go grab my purse and put my shoes on and we can go."

"Sounds good." I watch her walk out, her head held high and a confidence in her steps that shows she's willing to face whatever the day throws at her. Even when she's scared, she's strong.

I put the mug I'd grabbed back in the cupboard and then pull out two tumblers. I dump her coffee in one and then finish making mine. By the time I walk out to the foyer, she's taking the last step down the stairs, ready to go.

The drive to her apartment is long due to morning traffic. The closer we get, the more I can feel her tensing up in the passenger seat. By the time we pull up to her apartment complex, she's practically vibrating with nervous energy. I park and look around, understanding why Drew was nervous the day Emma moved in. The neighborhood doesn't look bad, but it has a vibe about it. Her apartment building looks like it recently got a new coat of paint, but that's about it.

Emma and I get out of the car and walk in silence toward her apartment. Even from a distance, I can tell the handrail is rusty and the doors are dirty. They look like a swift breeze would pop them right open leaving very little security for the tenants inside. When we get to the stairs, I look in every nook and cranny, my body strung tight and ready to protect her from any unseen danger. I pull her behind me as we start up the steps. She looks at me, confused by my behavior.

"No way in hell am I letting you go up first. Which apartment is it?" Her eyes soften and her shoulders fall slightly from their tense position by her ears as she points to the door up the stairs to the left. I take her hand in mine and pull her close to my back as we make our way up.

Holding her hand is a mistake.

If I wasn't aware of her before, I sure as fuck am now.

Her sweet scent wraps around me, and I have to actively fight to stay focused on the task at hand.

As soon as I approach the last step, I see her door still cracked open, and suddenly the only thought in my mind is to protect her at all costs. I slowly push the door open all the way, the creaking of the hinges sounding ominous to my ears.

I turn back to her. "Stay right behind me, okay?"

Her green eyes pierce me. "I could just stay here by the door," she whispers.

"No way. I'm not letting you out of my sight until we know this place is safe."

"Okay," she says softly, the corners of her lips turning up ever so slightly in a grateful smile.

I work my way slowly through her apartment, opening every door to make sure no one is hiding anywhere. Once I've done a full sweep and I'm convinced no one else is here, I finally look around and catalog the damage. Emma walks past me and goes straight to the bedroom. I follow her, stepping over clothes tossed around the room.

She sags to the floor and lets out a sob. I immediately run over to her, squatting down to see her lovingly tracing her fingers over a guitar, the strings loose and the neck broken. It looks like someone might've stepped on it.

I glance at Emma to see tears pouring down her now bright red cheeks. My heart clenches painfully in my chest at the despair on her face.

"Emma?" I say softly.

"My grandma bought me this guitar. She was the first person who ever really believed in me."

I look at the guitar with new understanding. Her grandma stood up for her when Drew and I were too little to understand how her parents were treating her. It didn't take Drew long to catch on that he was treated differently, and he immediately became Emma's biggest advocate and defender. Emma used to sing into spatulas when their grandma would come over and watch all of us kids. I'd never seen Emma as happy as she was when her grandma gifted her with a guitar for her eighth birthday. I can't believe she still has it. She clearly took care of it because despite the break and the messed-up strings, it looks like it's in pretty decent condition.

"Drew believes in you," I remind her.

She nods her head and sniffles. "I know. He's the only person, now that my grandma's gone. My parents are refusing to talk to me until I come to my senses." She rolls her eyes and shakes her head.

I didn't know that. I knew they were pissed about her decision not to pursue business, but I had no idea they'd stopped talking to her altogether. I'm surprised Drew never told me. I look a little more closely at Emma and realize maybe we have more in common than I thought. More than just Drew.

My parents never supported my pursuit of football. When I got drafted—hell, even when we won the Super Bowl last season—they still didn't believe in me. They regularly ask what my backup plan is if I get injured and can't play anymore. I actually think they hope I do get injured so that I'll go into business with my father, which was always his plan for me. Thank God football saved me from that fate.

Emma's vibrant green eyes stare up at me, and I feel another chunk of my resolve crumbling. "This was the only thing of value here."

I glance over at her dresser, noticing her jewelry box knocked over and mostly empty. I know for a fact she had expensive jewelry from her parents. Drew used to complain about his parents always nagging her to wear it when it so clearly wasn't her.

My respect for her grows. How many people who come from our affluent background would be more concerned about an old broken guitar than thousands of dollars' worth of jewelry?

"I can fix it," I say, my heart breaking the longer I have to watch her cry over her guitar.

Her head whips around, and her whispered word comes out breathy and hopeful. "What?"

"Well, not me." I hold up my hands. "I'm all thumbs, but a buddy of mine on the team is friends with a musician, and I bet he'd know a good person to take it to so we can get it fixed."

Her lip wobbles, her eyes filling with more tears, and I plead with her. "Emma, please don't cry. I told you last night, I'm shit with tears." Fuck, I'll text my teammate Will Edmonson right now to give me Trent Bridger's contact info if it'll get her to stop crying.

She huffs out a laugh as a tear escapes down her cheek. "Sorry, I'm a crier, Luke. You should probably get used to it."

She turns back and works on getting all the parts in her guitar case and collecting the rest of her personal items while her words jingle around in my head.

I don't need to get used to her crying because she won't be sticking around long enough for it to matter.

Even if the tiniest part of me wishes she could.

SEVEN

Emma

"Emma."

His breath whispers across my skin, and I blink my eyes open to see Luke sitting on the bed next to me. His heated gaze dances over my exposed skin, and it's then I realize I'm naked—weird because I swore I went to sleep in the same comfy cotton shorts and loose T-shirt combo I always wear.

I sit up, holding the sheet to my naked chest. "Is everything okay?"

He shakes his head, and the movement of his tongue sliding across his lower lip catches my gaze.

"Luke?" My voice is whisper soft. I'm afraid to hope that he's here for more than just a midnight chat.

He leans forward, his lips barely a breath from mine. "When did you get so beautiful?"

My heart flutters, and my stomach tightens as need courses swiftly through my body. I have no words for him, so I just stare at him, hoping he'll keep talking.

He lifts his hand and brushes a lock of my curly red hair away from my face. He leans closer to my ear and whispers, "So sexy," before placing a soft kiss against my smooth skin.

Oh, God. I think I might come if he does that again.

My body is strung tight, wanting him and desperate for him to take the lead.

"I've wanted you for so long," he mumbles against my neck, leaving another tender kiss that causes my sex to pulse rapidly and my breaths to come out in gentle pants.

"You have?" My voice is hoarse.

I can't believe this is happening.

He nods and trails his mouth along my jaw before pulling away just enough to look me in my eyes.

"You were always meant to be mine."

"Yes," I whisper, never breaking eye contact.

In the blink of an eye, his mouth is on mine in a kiss so possessive I know I will never belong to anyone else.

My hands grip his strong, corded biceps, holding him for dear life as he kisses me breathless. His tongue slides across mine erotically, causing my core to tighten in response. The kiss feels endless and is everything I've ever wanted.

I don't want to lose this feeling of belonging while he has me wrapped in his arms.

The blaring of an alarm causes me to pull away from him.

"What's that?"

He stands up from the bed, his expression cold and distant. "You didn't think I'd actually choose you, did you?"

"What?"

My eyes snap open to stare at the white ceiling as my heart races in my chest.

Holy shit.

I grab my beeping phone off the nightstand and slide my finger across the dismiss button before letting it fall to the bed while I try to steady my breath.

It was just a dream.

My fingers delicately graze my lips, which felt puffy and

well-used in my dream but feel completely normal now. God, it felt so real.

I roll over and groan into the bedspread in sexual frustration. I really need to have sex. Another groan releases because, let's be real, I won't be having sex at all while I'm living under the same roof as my dream man—the same one who's completely unattainable to me.

I roll back over as his last words in my dream filter through the sexual fog. My heart clenches painfully in my chest at the truth of his words.

Luke would never choose me over my brother. Even in my dreams, he doesn't choose me.

With one more groan, I stumble out of bed and into the shower, hoping the hot water and steam will rejuvenate me and ease some of this longing and heartache that is lingering from my dream.

When I make it down to breakfast, Luke is already gone, probably to practice or something else football related. That man lives and breathes football. While I make my coffee, I absently wonder if he still puts a penny in his shoe on game day or listens to a Britney Spears playlist before the game. I definitely wasn't supposed to know that information, but my brain is filled with secondhand knowledge about him from eavesdropping on him and Drew growing up.

But five years is a long time. I know I'm not the girl he once knew. Is Luke the same man he always was?

"Wait, so you're telling me you now live with Luke Carter? Running back for the Wolves. Man of my fucking dreams, Luke Carter?"

I nod.

Bernie throws her arms and legs out, held up only by her chair while she silently freaks out. "Girl, you won the freaking roommate lottery!"

I laugh. "Yeah, now if I could only make him see me as anything other than Drew's little sister. Not to mention, he's seen me in all my awkward glory. You have no idea how horrible I looked growing up." I pull out my phone and find an old Instagram picture of me.

Bernie looks at it, then slides her eyes up and down my body, raising her eyebrows and shaking her head. "Well, hun, you totally Neville Longbottomed, so he'd have to be an idiot or blind not to notice you."

Squinting, I ask, "Did you just reference Harry Potter?"

She smirks. "Honey, I'm a Hufflepuff for life. Don't you mock my obsession with Harry Potter."

"Not mocking at all. I just never would've expected that." I throw my hands up in a surrendering gesture.

"I waited for my Hogwarts letter for years and even tried to convince my parents that a giant mistake had been made because I was way too cool to be a muggle."

"How'd they take that?"

She looks affronted. "They told me Hogwarts couldn't handle me." Wiping a nonexistent tear in dramatic fashion, she says, "*Anyway*...back to your sexy roommate." She fans herself. "I still can't believe you live with Luke Carter." She shoots up out of her chair and grabs my arm. "Oh. My. God. Can you get me an introduction to Matt Fischer? He's so effing sexy."

I laugh. "I have no idea. I've only been living with Luke for a day. I haven't had any time to meet any of his friends. Besides, how will your boyfriend feel about you wanting to hook up with Matt Fischer?"

She waves away my question and sits back in her seat. "Matt's on my hall pass."

"Your what now?"

"Yeah, you know, the list of people you're allowed to sleep with if you ever meet them in real life. But that's beside the point right now." She leans forward conspiratorially. "Do you know how you're going to seduce Luke?"

I shake my head and roll my eyes at her. "I haven't the faintest idea. I've been secretly in love with him pretty much my entire life. If he hasn't noticed me already, then I don't know what it'll take."

Bernie gets a mischievous look in her eye that scares me a little. "I have some ideas. What are you doing tomorrow night?"

This is the dumbest thing I've ever done.

"I look like Sandy from *Grease*," I say, staring at myself in the mirror.

Bernie nods. "The hot Sandy. Hun, your ass was made for black leather pants. And your boobs in that crop top look fucking scrumptious. I'd bang you, and I'm straight as a flagpole. If that man doesn't swallow his tongue when he sees you walk out of here, then I'd question if he's even into women."

Nerves crash in my stomach like rocks in a cement mixer as anxiety and excitement battle for dominance. I fluff up my red hair that falls in soft waves along my shoulders and rub my signature red lips together before I step away and do another full body look in the mirror.

"Okay, let's do this. I'm as ready as I'm gonna get."

"Don't worry. I've got some other ideas if this doesn't get him to react."

"I feel like you're my wicked fairy godmother," I say with a laugh in my voice. Bernie just shrugs and offers me a coy smile before exiting my bedroom with me close on her heels. We make our way down the stairs, me taking my time in these sky-high heels. I rarely wear heels this high because I don't like towering over my dates, and they're usually only an inch or two taller than my five-foot, eight-inch frame.

But that's not something I need to worry about if I'm trying to get Luke to notice me.

"Emma? Is that you?" Luke calls from the kitchen.

Bernie turns to me, her brows furrowed, and whispers, "Who else would it be?"

I fight back another laugh and then call out, "Yeah, it's me." I head to the kitchen, admiring Luke's back in his fitted navy blue T-shirt and how his gray sweatpants hug his perfectly sculpted ass. Captain America has nothing on Luke Carter.

I bite my lip, which is a poor substitute for what I really want to bite into.

He turns around as he speaks. "Did you want to—"

Everything slows down as I watch his eyes start at my four-inch heels and move up my black leather-covered legs over the high waist of my pants. His gaze continues over the three inches of exposed midriff before my blood-red top starts and wraps around my breasts like it was made for them. It's got a deep V plunge that accentuates my already generous cleavage. His lidded hazel eyes finally meet mine, and the longing there nearly slams me against the wall.

He licks his lips and my body heats, a lightning bolt of desire shooting straight to my core that has my panties already dampening.

Fuck me sideways. I have *never* had a man look at me like he wanted to devour me on the spot. But that is exactly the way Luke is looking at me right now. I feel like Little Red Riding Hood with the big bad wolf coming to eat her.

The slickness between my thighs intensifies just thinking about how Luke could ravage me.

"I could cut the sexual tension between you two with a knife," Bernie whispers in my ear. My eyes never leave Luke's, but I slowly nod my head, acknowledging her words.

Luke jolts back, and the hooded look that was just in his eyes evaporates. In its place is shock and what looks a little like horror. My heart that had been soaring during our stare-off now falls hard into the depths of my stomach, cracking at how he shakes his head, runs his hands through his hair, and then escapes the room mumbling something about having plans with the guys tonight.

Bernie steps in front of me, her eyes wide with excitement. "Girl, he is totally feeling you."

I offer her a small smile. "Maybe." I have my doubts after witnessing his reaction. I don't think he could've rushed out of here faster even if his ass was on fire. "Even if he does, he'll never let himself follow through with it. He'll probably never even openly acknowledge it."

"Why the hell not?" she asks, completely put out by my pessimistic attitude.

One word. "Drew."

She doesn't understand. Luke and my brother have been inseparable since they were born. That term cradle to grave feels like it was invented for their friendship. I was so envious of their bond growing up. Drew and I are close, but I know his bond with Luke is even stronger and more unbreakable. I'd always wondered what it would be like to be that close to someone, but none of my own friendships ever came anywhere near what Luke and Drew had. I think Bernie might be the closest I've ever had to a best friend outside of my brother.

Luke and Drew got even closer—who knew that was possible—their sophomore year of college. I've suspected for a long time that something happened that year, but Drew never talked about it, which at the time was odd because I could usually get all his secrets out of him.

My brother has always been aware of my crush on Luke. He used to tease me about it when Luke wasn't around until he realized it was a very serious, I'm-in-love-with-your-friend crush. Then when he was eighteen and I was fourteen, he sat me down and told me that he loved me, but my crush on Luke was never going to go anywhere. Not only would Luke never see me that way, but Drew would never be okay with me dating his best friend. It would be too weird for him and change things between him and Luke.

My brother seemed crushed by that idea, so I tried to hide my feelings after that. Drew needed Luke. He never complained about the pressure my parents put on him, but I knew that Luke kept him grounded and gave him strength to become who he wanted to be and not just what my parents wanted for him. But I've never forgotten that conversation.

And clearly my brother was right if the look of horror on Luke's face just now was any indication. My feelings will never be reciprocated.

With one last glance up the stairs toward where Luke disappeared to, I tell Bernie, "Let's go."

The club Bernie takes me to is packed wall to wall with pretty people. I feel like I just stepped into a stereotypical movie about the small-town girl who moves to LA. Although, I grew up in Seattle, which is by no means a small town. Still, this place is hopping and clearly one of the trendiest clubs in LA. We've already seen four different celebrities, and we've only been here five minutes.

Bernie pushes her chest out as she gets closer to the bar. I fight back a smile as I watch her eye a hot blond guy next to her. When he offers to buy her a drink, she turns to me and arches her eyebrow. "I still got it."

I laugh and then bow down to her jokingly.

"Unfortunately for you, handsome, I have a boyfriend. But my girl here is single." He looks over at me, his gaze sliding salaciously over my body, clearly liking what he sees. I step closer to them and let the guy buy us both drinks. Two seconds after our drinks arrive, he tells us he's an entertainment lawyer, and starts name-dropping like no one's business. The second the word lawyer comes out of his mouth, my eyes glaze over.

Yeah, no thanks.

If I wanted to date a lawyer, doctor, or other corporate type, I would go home and let my parents set me up with their friends' sons like they've been dying to.

Lawyer guy glances to the left, catching the eye of a tall, beautiful blonde, and sensing my disinterest, he moves toward her. I look around the club, my body naturally swaying to the beat of the music. The DJ's doing a kick-ass job mixing, and I really want to get out there and dance. This isn't the type of music I write and sing, but I still appreciate it.

I lean toward Bernie and shout in her ear to be heard over the music, "I'm gonna go dance."

She holds up her pointer finger in the universal symbol to wait, downs her drink, and then pushes me toward the dance floor.

It's too loud to talk in here, but we don't need to as we both dance and sway to the beat. When two guys approach us, we dance with them for a while before I'm desperate for some water.

"I need agua!" I shout.

"Buddy system," Bernie shouts back. She grabs my hand, and we make our way through the pulsing bodies back toward the bar. I bump into a tall, fit body covered in a pair of black designer jeans and a white T-shirt that perfectly hugs his sculpted biceps while falling loosely over his tapered waist. This man's outfit may say casual, but when my eyes rove over the fine details, I can spot the designer logos that tell me this guy is loaded. My hand lands on his chest, and my gaze slides up to meet piercing blue eyes.

"I'm so sorry. I didn't mean to bump into you," I yell.

He gives me a charming smile. "You can bump into me anytime." He winces and leans down to whisper in my ear, "Shit, I didn't mean for that to come out like a corny line."

I smile at him, instantly at ease with how he called himself out. Bernie tugs my hand, just now noticing I've stopped. "I have to go."

He looks over at Bernie. "Why don't you two join me up there?" He points to one of the VIP boxes on the second floor.

I look over at Bernie and then back at him. Fuck it, why not? "Sure. We're just grabbing some water. We'll meet you there."

He smiles that sexy smile and then heads toward the stairs.

I take the few steps to get within hearing distance of Bernie and shout, "He wants us to join him in his VIP box."

Her eyes go wide, and a smile lifts her cheeks. "Yeah, girl. Okay, let's hustle and get these drinks."

The VIP box is very high-end, and the sound from the main floor is muted so you can still hear it, but you can also have a conversation without having to yell. Bernie and I quickly find out that my tall, dark, and handsome's name is Jason, and he's a music producer.

"Get the fuck out!" Bernie points at me. "My girl here is an incredible singer. Like you'd-be-stupid-not-to-work-with-her incredible."

I can't stop the blush staining my fair cheeks. The curse of red hair—my skin always gives away what I'm feeling.

Jason turns heated eyes on me. "Is that right?"

"It is."

"What kind of music do you sing?"

I'm prepared for this. "I write my own. My sound is a mix between Florence and the Machine, Julia Michaels, and Ella Henderson."

His eyebrows lift. "I'd really like to hear that."

My heart beats excitedly. Could this be my chance to make my dreams finally come true?

Jason reaches into his pocket and grabs a pen off the table. He scribbles on the back and then hands me his business card. "That's my personal cell number. Give me a call, and we'll set up a meeting to talk about your career."

"I'd love that."

When Bernie and I leave the club a few hours later, I'm feeling lighter than when we got there, and not because of the number of drinks we had but because things are finally starting to turn around for me. I'm one step closer to reaching my dreams. Now, if only I could make my dream about a certain Wolves player come true.

EIGHT

Luke

Keeping Emma at arm's length has been harder than I expected. I've been forced to find as many activities to stay out of the house as possible.

I can't believe I've been driven out of my own damn house by the girl who used to collect what she called potato bugs as pets and refused to call them roly-polies when everyone knows that's what they're actually called. They don't even look like a potato.

God, why am I even thinking about that stupid memory? Fuck, she's messing with my head, and she doesn't have a clue. I thought maybe my house would be safe when she's at work, but her scent is everywhere. The soft lilac fragrance permeates it and will hit me out of nowhere when I'm just trying to mind my own damn business. Just that one smell and I'm lost to thoughts I one hundred and fifty percent should NOT be having.

I've never been so thankful to have the excuse of an away game.

We won our game against the Steelers, and now I'm out celebrating with a bunch of guys on the team. The Fierce Four —Gabe Romero, Romel Watson, Dominic Smith, and Tyler

Russell—are bunched a few seats to my right. Will just went to the bathroom. Jack Fuller, our quarterback, already went back to the hotel to call his fiancée, and I'm pretty sure Matt didn't even bother coming out.

Matt's acting weird and evasive lately. I wish I knew what was going on with him. He's always been a pretty easygoing guy —cocky, confident, driven, and a total ladies' man. But something has changed lately. I've asked him more than once what's going on, and I feel like a fucking broken record. I'm not used to my friends keeping secrets from me. Drew and I have always been honest with each other about everything.

Which definitely only adds to my frustration and guilt when it comes to this insane attraction I feel toward his sister.

My loyalty is to Drew.

I repeat the mantra in my head until I feel a hand on my left arm. I glance up from where I was staring at my beer on the bar counter to see a beautiful brunette perched on the stool next to me.

"Is this seat taken?"

I toss her a friendly smile. "Nope, all yours."

She crosses her leg, angling her body toward me. I know the move well, and under normal circumstances I would be engaging her in a conversation that would hopefully end up with me buried inside her by the end of the night.

But I have zero interest. There's not a single flutter of excitement in my gut or slight pulse in my dick. Nothing. Nada. Zilch.

Maybe I need to lay off the booze. I mean, I've only had one beer, but that has to be the problem, right?

I refuse to believe it could be anything else.

I grip the back of my neck and glance over at the very sexy brunette who bats her lashes at me and gives me a flirty smile. Maybe I should try to pursue this anyway. Getting laid might help me stop thinking about Emma. And this woman is giving me all the signs that say she's looking for a good time.

But the idea of fucking her when Emma's been owning all the thoughts in my brain makes me feel a little queasy—and maybe even a little too much like my dad. When I'm with a woman, my sole focus is on her, and as much as I loathe to admit it to myself, that wouldn't be the case tonight.

A hand slaps my back, and I glance up at Will standing near the stool on my right that he vacated a few minutes ago. "You getting another beer, or you thinking of heading back to the hotel soon?"

I look at my nearly empty beer and see the brunette shift in my periphery. The movement causes her dress to move up her leg, exposing more of her smooth, tan thighs. She clears her throat just as I'm about to respond to Will and places her delicate hand back on my arm.

"You should stay," she says in a sultry voice.

No. I should definitely go. In one large gulp, I down the rest of my beer and stand, turning to Will. "Let's head back."

Will's a pretty stoic guy, always has been, so it doesn't surprise me that he doesn't ask about the brunette or why I'm brushing her off when she is very clearly a sure thing.

What does surprise me is how badly I want to talk about it with him. We exit the bar into the cold night air and start walking. Our hotel is only a couple of blocks away.

"Have you ever been interested in someone you shouldn't be interested in?" The words tumble out of my mouth before my brain has a chance to stop them. Normally, I would talk to Drew about this kind of thing, but that's a big no for obvious reasons, and I can't talk to Matt because he's clearly got something else going on, so Will's the next best thing.

"Who are you interested in?"

"It's a hypothetical question."

He arches a brow. "Uh-huh."

I huff out a breath and watch it blow out of my mouth. It's so damn cold my nipples could cut glass. Why is Pittsburgh so fucking cold in the winter?

I cave, because I need to get this off my chest, and let the words spill out. "You know my best friend, Drew?"

"Yeah, the lawyer who hangs out with us when he comes to visit?"

"Yeah. Well, his sister moved down here from Seattle to pursue a singing career."

He lets out a whistle. "That's a tough gig in LA."

"Yeah, no shit. Well, she rented out this apartment that she thought would be fine but turned out to be massively sketchy, and the next thing I know she's living with me. And she's making me coffee in the mornings, and she looks nothing like I fucking remember. I mean, she was an awkward kid. She had the whole freckle-faced, carrot top, four-eyes thing down pat, and then she shows up looking like a goddamn knockout, and I can't fucking sleep or eat or even be in my own house." I stop in my tracks and finally take a damn breath. Grabbing his arm, I add, "She's driven me out of my own damn house, man."

Will's face contorts for a split second before he keels over laughing his ass off. My shoulders sag in disbelief. This asshole is seriously laughing at me right now. I'm living in hell, and he's fucking laughing.

"Are you for real, man? This is not a laughing matter!"

He raises his hand and shakes his head. Tears form at the corners of his eyes while I just stand there in dismay. Finally, he heaves in a couple of deep breaths and stands up straight again.

"Okay, okay, sorry." He clears his throat, trying—and failing—to find complete composure. With a glimmer in his eye, he says, "So, you finally found a woman who knocked you off your axis."

"That's not what's happening."

"That's what it sounds like to me."

"No. I don't like Emma." I don't. I can't. "I'm just thrown because it's been five years since I last saw her, and she looks completely fucking different. I'm only human, so of course I'd find her attractive, right? That's a normal response."

Will just smiles at me, which does not make me feel better.

"You have sisters. How would you feel if one of your friends was attracted to one of them?"

He shrugs. "Depends on the friend and his intentions."

My jaw drops a little. I wasn't expecting that answer. I was expecting a firm no. It's bro code. You do not date your friend's sister.

"You're telling me you'd be okay with one of your friends— let's just say your *best friend*—dating your sister?"

"Like I said, it depends on his intentions. If he's just using her, then no, I wouldn't be okay with that. But if he cared about her and they were genuinely trying to make a go of it, then sure, why not?"

"Because he's your best friend!"

He frowns at me. "Yeah, which means I know he's a good guy. I'm not friends with assholes. Why would I have a problem with my sister dating someone who I know will treat her right?"

I stare at him in absolute shock. He's so sure about his response that it has me questioning if Drew would respond as well as Will has.

What would Drew say if I admitted the truth to him? If I admitted that I find his sister attractive? I think about Will's response long after we part ways into our individual hotel rooms. One word keeps circling around my brain.

Intentions.

Will said he'd be fine with it as long as his friend's intentions were good.

I know I'm attracted to Emma, but it's been five years since I've seen her, and while I've known her my entire life, I don't really *know* her.

I need to figure out what my intentions are with Emma. Is this just some weird attraction because it's been too long since I was in a relationship? Or could this be more?

Only one way to find out.

NINE

Emma

"Can you pass the Skittles?"

I bend over, reaching for the bowl of Skittles on the coffee table in Luke's giant living room. Bernie is lounging on the other end of his sectional as *10 Things I Hate About You* plays on his big screen TV.

When he said he was going out of town for an away game, I figured that was the perfect opportunity for a girls' night—something Bernie and I have been talking about for a while.

"Thanks," she says when I hand her the bowl. "So, how long will Luke be away for?"

"Just a day or two, I think, not that it feels all that different from when he's here."

"What do you mean?"

"I mean, Luke's never around." I turn my body toward Bernie and pull my knees up to my chest as I lean on the armrest. "Drew made it sound like he was kind of a homebody, but he's rarely ever here. It's like he finds some excuse to leave whenever I'm home, which admittedly is most of the time since I've been working on more music, and I prefer to do that in private." I nibble my lip. "I feel like he's avoiding me in particular."

Bernie turns her body so she's facing me, her legs criss-crossed. "Why would he be avoiding you?"

"I have no idea. Unless…"

She raises her brows in anticipation. "Unless what?"

I cover my face and groan before answering. "Unless he's caught on that I still have a crush on him. Maybe this is just his polite way of brushing me off until I find a new place."

She tilts her head and stares up at the ceiling, clearly thinking hard. "What if it's something else? What if he's just busy? I mean, it is football season, and don't players always have sponsorships and shit that they have to juggle on top of practices and games?"

"You think I'm just overreacting?"

She shrugs. "You could be. Give it more time. You've only been living with him for a couple of weeks."

"That's true. It wouldn't be the first time I've overreacted."

She smiles at me with understanding in her eyes. "Girl, I feel that."

We turn back toward the TV and watch the movie for a bit before Bernie speaks without looking away from the screen.

"Kat Stratford always made being the outcast look cool. She's such a badass who doesn't give a shit what anyone thinks of her, but that's not always reality."

"What do you mean?" I ask, munching on some popcorn.

"I mean, sometimes being the outcast can be really lonely. When your family doesn't understand you or puts you down because you're different from them, it can make you feel like no one in the world will ever get you."

I stare at her, my jaw dropped. It's like she's in my head. "And like maybe there's something wrong with you."

She turns to me, and I know in this moment our friendship just solidified itself even further. She nods.

"My parents think I'm wasting my time pursuing music. They've hardly spoken to me since I moved here because they're mad at me," I confess.

Her gaze is sympathetic. "I haven't talked to my family in five years."

Bernie's my age, so that means she hasn't talked to her family since she was seventeen. "What happened?"

Her eyes get glassy, and her voice has the slightest catch when she says, "That's a long, depressing story."

I can tell she doesn't want to talk about it, and I don't want to push her if she's not ready.

"You were only seventeen. Where did you live?"

She drops her gaze down to her hands resting in her lap. "I moved in with JJ. He and I were dating, and his parents were never around, so I just secretly moved in with him and then when we turned eighteen, we got our own place together."

"And you've been together ever since."

She nods but still doesn't look up. She doesn't talk a whole lot about her boyfriend, but what she does share makes him sound more like a friend than a boyfriend.

"Do you love him?"

"I don't believe in love."

"What? How is that possible?"

She looks up at me now, and I see tears pooling in her eyes, but she brushes them away before they have a chance to fall down her face. "I've never seen love except what's depicted in movies or books. My parents got married because they thought that's what you do when you get knocked up at sixteen. I don't think they ever loved each other, but they're both too stubborn and determined to prove their own parents wrong so they won't divorce each other. Instead, they've stayed in a loveless marriage where they can barely stand the other. They even sleep in separate rooms.

"When JJ and I got together, I was attracted to his drive to succeed, but then we moved in together and he just gave up. He works at a gas station making minimum wage, and when he comes home, he just plays video games. But he treats me well. He's nice to me. He doesn't nitpick my life, and the sex is still pretty good, so I don't see any point in changing the status quo."

She shrugs and turns her head back to the TV, but her eyes have that faraway look that tells me she's not actually seeing what's on the screen.

I stare at her, still too shocked to move. That's the most she's ever shared about her family, and I have a million follow-up questions—about both her family and JJ—but I get the sense if I push, she'll shut down. Instead, I crawl across the couch and wrap her up in a big hug. She's stiff for a second before she lets out a sigh and sags into my hug, her arm reaching up to hug me back.

"Thank you for sharing that with me."

She gives me a small smile, and then I move back to my seat, and we continue watching the movie.

Drew's name flashes on my screen. "Hey, D. You have good timing. I'm on a break at work."

"Great. I was hoping I could catch you since it's been a few days. I've been slammed with this case."

"No worries. What's up?"

"I was just calling to check in and see how you're settling into LA. Any leads on a new place?"

"I'm looking, but so far nothing. All the apartments I've found are either out of my budget or in a shady part of town. I found one place I loved, but there were like ten other people who applied for it, so I didn't get it. Bernie has a friend who might be subletting her place soon, and that has potential, but I won't know for a few weeks."

"Well, keep me posted. Everything going okay with Luke? He hasn't called me complaining yet, so I'm guessing you two are getting along okay." He says it with a laugh, but my stomach clenches because I know the real reason he hasn't complained.

"He's actually never home."

"What?" He laughs in disbelief. "Luke's always home when he's not on the road."

I nibble my lip. Drew's not making me feel any better about the doubts I already had. In fact, he's just confirmed I was right.

"I think maybe he's avoiding me."

There's silence on the other end before Drew responds, all hint of laughter completely gone. "Did you say or do something? Because Luke loves his house. You don't still have that damn crush on him, do you? I thought we talked about that years ago."

I ignore his comment about my crush. It's the one secret I've kept from him since that conversation. "I didn't do anything. He's just not been around. Maybe you should ask him."

"Maybe I will."

"Good."

"Yeah, it is." He groans. "Okay, how old are we, because that felt a little too high school for comfort."

I let out a laugh. "We're siblings. Do we ever truly get over having the occasional immature fight?"

"I wouldn't say that was a fight."

I glance at the clock. "Fair, but I gotta go. I'll call you later, okay?"

"Sounds good, Squish. Love you."

"Love you too, D."

I hang up and head out to the bustling restaurant. I try to

stay focused on my customers and orders, but my conversation with my brother keeps cycling through my mind.

As the night wears on, I come to two definite conclusions. Luke is definitely avoiding me, and he hasn't talked to my brother about it. But those conclusions only lead to a slew of questions. Why wouldn't Luke talk to Drew? They tell each other everything. Is it possible I did something that made Luke uncomfortable?

But most importantly, if I did do something, how am I going to fix it?

TEN

Luke

On the drive home from the airport, I get stuck in traffic and decide to call Drew. My conversation with Will has been on a non-stop loop in my head, and I need to talk to my best friend or I'm going to go crazy. I have to feel him out first before I spend more time with Emma. The last thing I need is to fall deeper into whatever the hell is going on with me only to have Drew shut it down.

He picks up on the fourth ring. "Hey, man."

"Dude, you sound wiped."

"Yeah, this case...it's kicking my ass," he says with a heavy sigh.

"Maybe you should hook up with that hot paralegal who's got a wicked crush on you and blow off some steam."

He huffs out a laugh. "Yeah, no. I don't fuck where I eat—or work, in this case. It's that whole don't shit where you eat thing."

My gut clenches a little because I'm pretty sure he'd think me wanting to hook up with his sister is the exact definition of shitting where you eat. I need to approach this very carefully.

Before I have a chance to talk, he speaks first. "I talked to Emma last night. She said you've hardly been home." His tone changes, and I pick up on a slight hesitation. "Are you avoiding her?"

How do I answer that? I mean, yes, I'm avoiding her, but if he's picked up on that after talking to her, does that mean *she* knows I'm avoiding her? Fuck, I don't want her to feel like I'm trying to stay away from her, even if it's the truth. She'll probably think I'm staying away because I don't want to be around her when it's the exact opposite reason.

I must pause for too long because he lets out a heavy sigh. "Fuck, I was worried about this. She did something awkward, didn't she? You know I love my sister, but I won't take it personally if you tell me she's too much."

"She's not too much."

He hesitates. "Then why haven't you been home? And don't give me any bullshit excuse because you and I both know you're a homebody when you're not working or away for games."

How much do I tell him? I've never been in this position before. I've never held back the complete truth from him, and I don't like doing it now, but I feel like I'm in a very precarious situation.

"Emma's fine. She's just...not what I was expecting."

There's a pause before he says, "What do you mean?" There's caution in his voice, almost like he's dreading my answer.

"She doesn't look like I remember, and I just wasn't expecting her to look so...well, to be honest, man, your sister got fucking hot."

There's a moment of silence before he says, "No." His voice is hard, brooking no argument. But I push back anyway.

"What do you mean 'no'?"

"You cannot have the hots for my sister. Absolutely not. It's bro code." He sighs heavily, but when he speaks, there's a vulnerability in his voice that I'm not sure I've ever heard from him before. "Please tell me you're just fucking with me right now."

I know Drew, probably better than anyone else—even himself sometimes—and I know the only answer he'll accept.

"Uh, yeah." I'm not that convincing, but it's what he wants to hear, so he doesn't question it.

"Thank God, because it would seriously fuck with our friendship if you hooked up with my sister. Especially if things went south with you two. I can't deal with that. I don't want to be put in the position where I have to choose sides."

My gut clenches. I hadn't thought about things not working out. I mean, who goes into a relationship with the end already in mind? But he's right. If I did act on how I've been feeling and things didn't work out, it would be hard for all of us. My life is so intertwined with Drew's. I'd have to see Emma at family events over the years, and if Drew ever settles down, I'd see her at his wedding.

He's right to say no. It's for the best that I don't follow through on these feelings.

"Hey, hold on a sec," he says. I can hear him murmuring to someone else before he comes back on the line. "Hey, I gotta get back to work, but we're all good, right?" There's that hint of vulnerability again.

"Yeah, man, we're good." The words leave a bad taste in my mouth because I'm dying a little inside knowing he's so adamantly opposed to the idea of me liking Emma.

We hang up so he can go back to work, and I spend the rest of the drive to my house lost in my thoughts. Clearly, Emma's on to my evasive routine, so I'm going to have to spend more time in my house with her. But Drew's comments made it clear that he would not be okay with me dating his sister. I need to find a way to be around Emma, keep her in the friend zone, and keep my dick from responding to her.

Should be a piece of cake.

Yeah, right.

My steps falter the second I near the kitchen and see Emma dancing around, her head bopping to a beat only she can hear coming from her headphones. She wasn't home when I got back last night, so I didn't have a chance to talk to her after my conversation with Drew. I step back around the corner, so I can watch her like the ginormous creep I'm turning into.

I don't understand what she's doing to me, but my concern over what her brother would think if he saw me right now evaporates as I watch her ass shake in her short cotton shorts that hug her in a way I didn't know cotton shorts could. The swooping neck of her oversized T-shirt slides off her left shoulder as she continues to shimmy around the room, humming a tune I recognize as "Don't Stop Believing" by Journey.

A soft smile breaks free as I continue to watch her in fascination. The gentle, rhythmic motions of her body are seductive, even if she doesn't intend for them to be. Well, they're seducing me at least.

My smile widens when she stops in the middle of the kitchen and sings into a spatula like she's putting on a performance at the Hollywood Bowl. I'm still trying to wrap my head around the fact this is the same girl I grew up around. She starts spinning around and doing an adorable shimmy that makes her ass jiggle deliciously, when she suddenly stops and throws her arms up in a flourish like she's Molly Shannon in *Superstar*.

Yep, the old Emma's still in there, I think with an intrigued smile still on my face.

I clap gently and step around the corner, causing her to immediately stand up straight and a gorgeous pink blush to spread across her face.

She bites her lip nervously and then gives me a wary expression. "How long were you standing there?"

I smile wide. Actually, I'm not sure I've stopped smiling since I first saw her in the kitchen, but I'm not going to fight it since I've decided I'm going to try to be friends with her. "Long enough to see you still remember the famous *Superstar* move."

A laugh breaks free from her chest as she covers her face, shaking her head at the same time. Then she looks at me unapologetically. "Well, I guess the cat's out of the bag. I'm still weird."

I walk by her, letting our arms brush in the process. "I always liked your brand of weird."

I don't miss her sharp inhale as her smile drops slightly and doubt fills her eyes. "No, you didn't."

"What makes you think I didn't?"

She leans against the counter next to me. "You always ignored me."

"Doesn't mean I didn't see you."

And fuck if that's not the truth. There was always something about Emma that demanded attention. It wasn't exactly attraction like it is now, but it was...something.

She just stares at me, her bottom lip captured between her teeth. I fight the urge to lean forward and see what it tastes like for myself.

My pants get tighter, and I turn my body away from her under the pretense of getting coffee, while discreetly adjusting myself.

No. Friend zone, asshole. She's off-limits.

She walks closer to the stove and focuses on cooking the eggs that I just now noticed in a pan.

I glance up at her, and she must feel the weight of my stare because she looks up, and her eyes instantly connect with mine. "I saw you too."

I know.

Her childhood crush on me wasn't a secret, just something I pretended not to notice. But I always noticed. I never felt anything for her romantically when we were growing up. We were too different. She was too young.

But she doesn't feel too young now.

I shake the thought from my head. I need to get out of here before I say—or worse, do—something I can't take back.

Ignoring the cup of coffee I just poured, I say, "I gotta head to practice. I'll see ya later." I rush out of the kitchen, grab my keys, and flee to the safety of my car. Maybe practice can knock some sense into me.

The sun beats on my back at our practice field as I jog over to the sidelines. Grabbing my water bottle, I take a hearty drink before dumping some on my head and face to help me cool off. Matt runs over and stands next to me drinking his own water. For what feels like the millionth time, I wonder what it'll take for him to open up to me about whatever's going on with him. I'm really starting to worry about him.

"How's the campaign going?" I ask, knowing he's had to work with Coach Denton's daughter on the latest Wolves campaign. It's a big honor, but he can't stand Nikki Denton, and she's the one running the whole thing. I believe "pampered ice princess" was what he called her. He's not wrong. She definitely comes off as cold and controlled.

He shrugs and looks off. "It's fine."

Annoyed with his brush-off, I lean down and ask, "You ever gonna tell me what's going on with you?"

He gets a look in his eye I'm not sure I've seen before, but then shakes his head. "I've told you I'm fine."

I burn a hole in the side of his head with my eyes before he finally turns to me. "What?"

"Why won't you tell me?"

"There's nothing to tell." He turns back to the field, but I catch his expression, and it's one I recognize well from seeing it staring back at me in my mirror lately—guilt.

What the hell could he be guilty about?

I decide not to push it, knowing he won't tell me if he doesn't want to.

"How's the new roommate?" he asks, changing the subject.

My back stiffens and my gut clenches. How do I even answer that?

She's driving me crazy?

She's hotter than sin?

She's totally, completely, one hundred percent off-limits?

All of the fucking above?

Borrowing his line, I reply, "It's fine."

Matt turns to me with a small smirk tipping up the corner of his lips. He nods his head knowingly and then drops his water bottle and hustles back to the field.

I take one more swig of water and run after him, hoping I can finally push away all the thoughts of Emma that seem to infiltrate every spare moment of my time these days. I can still picture her in those damn leather pants looking like a vintage pinup wet dream come to life.

Not to mention our interaction this morning. I swear my arm is still tingling from where we touched. Maybe I should see if the team doctor could take a look at that.

Despite her tempting attire, she's definitely already a better roommate than Drew ever was. That fucker only ever left dirty dishes in the sink and empty pizza boxes everywhere. She cleans up after herself and always leaves me leftovers for after practice.

Practice flies by, and my body aches in the best way by the time I get cleaned up and head home. I walk in the front door eager to relax and watch some game tape to prep for our next game.

Music hits my ears as I near the stairwell, the song soft and slow. The sound of her guitar reaches my ears, and I smile to myself. I had it fixed for her but haven't been around to hear her play.

I walk up the stairs, the lyrics becoming clearer the closer I get, about belonging to someone.

Tapping the door softly, I enter right as she finishes. "Hey."

"Hey," she responds, tucking a lock of her red hair behind her ear.

"That was pretty. Did you write it?"

"No. It's "Yours" by Ella Henderson. She's one of my favorites."

"I've never heard the original, but your version sounded really good."

She ducks her head, but I still catch her blush. "Thanks," she says.

I stand there awkwardly for a moment, not sure if I should stay and try to talk to her or leave. Leaving would definitely be the safe option, but I can't seem to force myself to walk away.

She looks up, and her bright green eyes land on mine. "Thank you for fixing my guitar. I've been meaning to thank you for a while, but you've been really busy. I can pay you back when I get my next paycheck."

Ignoring her comment about me being busy, I respond,

"Keep your money. It's a gift. You got a shit start to life in LA. It's the least I could do to turn things around for you."

"I think letting me live with you is already fulfilling that obligation," she says with a smirk, but her words make me frown.

"Helping you isn't an obligation." I hate that she thinks it is.

Her small smile falls, and she looks down at her guitar. "I know you're only doing it for Drew."

That might be how it started, but it's not the reason she's still here. Hell, if I was still doing this for Drew, I would've found her an apartment already or paid for her to stay in a nice hotel the second the first dirty thought about her filtered through my head.

No, letting her stay here is now for very selfish reasons.

I like her. More than I've liked any woman I can remember dating since Anna.

Fuuuck.

I take a breath. I need to turn this around. I can never pursue her, but we can be friends. I've never been friends with a woman before, but I'm sure I can figure it out.

I focus back on her. "You want to eat dinner and watch some bad TV?"

Her whole face lights up with her smile, and my heart stops in my chest as she looks at me with such joy. I wonder what it would take for me to always have her look at me like that.

Shit, I'm fucked.

ELEVEN

Emma

I walk into the house from my long shift at work and immediately head upstairs to my room to change into more comfy clothes. I opt for a pair of my short cotton booty shorts that make my legs look like they go on for days. I've always loved my legs. I may be on the curvier side, but my legs are toned and long and one of my favorite assets. I throw on a large scoop-neck sweater that hangs loosely off one of my shoulders. This style is one of my favorites for when I'm just relaxing at home. It's comfy but cute. According to Bernie, it's even a little seductive. She's been pressuring me more and more lately to seduce Luke, especially since he doesn't seem to be avoiding me anymore. It's only been a few days since he first invited me to eat dinner and watch TV with him, but he's been home more, and I'm taking that as a positive sign that maybe I didn't do something to drive him away after all.

But I'm on the fence about whether I should follow Bernie's advice or not. A small part of me—okay, a giant part—wants me to go through with her suggestion, because when will I ever get this chance again? This is the first time Luke and I have spent any amount of time together without Drew. I feel like if I don't take a chance now, then I have to let him go for good. The other, more sensible part of me is terrified of getting rejected and then having to deal with an angry Drew.

No, thanks.

But then I think about the advice my grandma used to give me about pursuing my music career. If you want something, you have to go after it. You'll always wonder "what if" if you don't, and a life with regrets isn't worth it.

Gazing at my reflection in the mirror, hearing her words float through my mind, I make a decision. Pulling off my sweater, I change into a tight tank top that makes my breasts look amazing and fluff my hair so it has that just-had-sex messy look. I touch up my signature red matte lipstick and then head downstairs. I stop by the kitchen and make a bowl of popcorn before walking into the living room and sitting next to Luke on the couch while game tape plays on the TV.

I can practically feel his gaze as it slides up my exposed legs, over my stomach, across my cleavage and finally on to my face. Victory thrums through my veins at the spark of desire in his eyes.

I hold the bowl of popcorn out to him, a silent offering that he takes while clearing his throat.

"Did you want to watch something?" he asks.

"With you?" I ask, my gaze focused on his while I put a piece of popcorn in my mouth. He follows the movement and swallows audibly before replying.

"Sure. I can watch this tomorrow." I get a little giddy at how throaty his voice is right now.

Pretending to be completely unaffected by our proximity, I say, "Okay, what do you want to watch?"

He hands me the remote. "Lady's choice."

I smirk and immediately start scrolling through Netflix looking at my options.

"I heard you playing your guitar this morning. Was that another Ella Henderson song?" he asks, passing the bowl of popcorn back to me.

Without taking my eyes off the TV, I take the bowl and reply, "No, that's an original. I met a producer when Bernie and I were out at that club last week, and he wants to meet with me and hear my stuff. He had to fly to New York for an album he's working on, but he will get in touch when he gets back."

Luke's body stiffens, and out of the corner of my eye, I can see him staring at me. I turn toward him, confused as to why he's frowning.

"What?" I ask.

"This guy approached you at a nightclub when you were dressed like hot Sandy?"

My body warms, my heart beats excitedly, and I blush as I realize he just implied he thought I looked hot. I mean, I figured, based on his reaction, but this is the first time he's acknowledged it.

He leans his head forward, clearly waiting for a response, and I realize he asked me a question. "Yeah, why?"

He shakes his head and looks back at the TV, but his jaw is clenched tight, and his hands are fisted at his side. "I don't like it. That's not how you do business, and it sounds sketchy as hell to me."

My heart sinks, and I instantly get defensive and protective of him shitting on a potential way to make my dream come true. "It's not sketchy."

He turns to me. "Did he even hear you sing?" His gaze slides down my body, but instead of feeling excited by his attention, I feel cold, waiting for him to pull the rug out from under me. "Or did he just take one look at you in that outfit and think you were an easy score?"

And there it is.

Does Luke really think so little of me?

Tears burn behind my eyes, but I hold them back. "So, someone can only give me a chance if they think I'm hot?"

"Did he actually hear you sing?" he asks again, slower. Before I can answer, he says, "I fucking doubt it. You were in a loud club. I know what you looked like that night, remember? I'm sure he's just looking to get laid." The disdain dripping from his voice turns my hurt into anger in the blink of an eye.

I stand and toss the bowl of popcorn on his lap, taking him by surprise.

"What the fuck, Emma?"

Turning to glare at him, I spit out, "Fuck you, Luke. Not that it's any of your goddamn business, but yes, he did hear me sing. I played him some of my stuff I had recorded on my phone, but it's nice to know you think I'd be so naïve, and that a man could only be interested in me for my body. Most people in this town would think the opposite since I'm not exactly a size zero." His mouth gapes like a fish out of water, but I continue before he can interrupt me. "I'm not stupid. I have a degree in business, and I know how this shit works. It's all about networking and who you know. But it's good to know I'm just a piece of ass. Go fuck yourself."

I turn around and rush up the stairs, engaging the lock as soon as the door is shut behind me. Once I'm in the safety of my room, the tears I'd been holding back downstairs fall in torrents down my face.

Fuck him.

Fuck him for thinking someone could only be interested in me because of how I look. I know this is LA, and it can be really superficial, but does he honestly think I'm that stupid and naïve?

Clearly, he does.

Again, fuck him.

I didn't even bother telling him that I googled the address Jason gave me and looked into him. He's one of the top producers in Hollywood. And even though I wasn't able to actually see what his studio looks like because Google Maps just shows a tall gate with lots of plants, I know Jason's the real deal from all the other information I was able to find about him. I'm even planning for Bernie to go with me as backup to make sure he keeps things professional.

A knock intrudes on my inner raging. "Emma?" At least he has the decency to sound remorseful.

I don't answer him. One, because I'm still mad at him, and he deserves to sit in his guilt for a bit longer. Two, because I'm silently sobbing, and I refuse to let him know he hurt my feelings this badly.

Sensitivity and emotion are great when I'm songwriting, but moments like this, I wish I had thicker skin. I wish what people thought of me didn't manage to seep through the armor I wear so carefully for the world. My vintage style and perfectly done makeup are all people tend to see, not the broken girl who just wants someone to love her for her.

The girl who wants to be enough, just as she is.

"Emma, I'm sorry. It was a dumb thing to say." His voice gets softer, closer, almost like he's leaning his head against the door. "Please come out. Or let me in. I'll take either one. I just need to know you're okay."

What about what I need?

I need someone who believes in me and supports my decisions, who trusts that I'm making good choices, and if I'm not, isn't a complete dick about telling me that's what he thinks.

I take another shuddering breath and wipe under my eyes. I can't open the door. He'll know I was crying. But I also can't keep avoiding him. I close my eyes and inhale deeply. I've had a lot of practice pulling myself together and composing my voice so others—primarily my parents—wouldn't know the power they had over my emotions.

"I'm fine, Luke," I say just loud enough for him to hear, afraid any louder might cause my voice to crack.

There's silence on the other side of the door. Did he already walk away? My heart sinks to my stomach, and disappointment courses through me.

"Open the door, Emma." His voice booms and sends a chill racing down my spine.

"No. I'm really fine. I'm going to bed."

"I swear to God, Em, if you don't open this door right now, I'll break it down."

I stare at the door, confused. Why does he sound mad? I'm the one who should be mad!

I unlock the door and turn the handle. My breath catches in my lungs at Luke's large imposing body as he leans his hands on the frame, his knuckles white. His hazel eyes immediately lock on mine, and I don't miss the pain in them as his gaze caresses my face, noting what I'm sure are red eyes and blotchy cheeks.

"I fucking knew it," he mumbles, dropping his head and taking a big breath before releasing his grip on the door frame and walking up to me. His strong arms wrap around me, and he pulls me against his body in a hug that has all my defenses crumbling completely.

"I'm so fucking sorry," he says, his mouth brushing against the top of my head. "I don't think you're stupid, Em, not at all." He pulls away and dips his head down so our eyes are at the same level. "I fucked up, but I also didn't mean it as a slight against you. Music producers can be really sleazy, and a lot of people get taken advantage of all the time. Listen, if you're going to meet with this producer, at least let me come with you as support, just to make sure he's on the up and up. Drew trusts me to look out for you, and I don't trust this guy's motives."

Drew.

Drew trusts him to look out for me.

My whole body shuts down as realization sweeps over me that this is all about Drew.

It's not about me at all.

Which might hurt even more than him thinking I'm a naïve little girl.

I put on my best face, smile softly at him because I know that's what he needs to feel forgiven, and feel my heart break a little more when he buys it, his returning smile a sign he thinks we're all good.

We're not.

Luke Carter has had my heart for far too long. No more.

Time to let him go.

TWELVE

Luke

Something's wrong with Emma, and I don't know how to fix it.

I am not a guy who does well feeling helpless. I like action, fixing things, making shit happen. But for a week, I've had to deal with Emma pulling away from me. Distancing herself every way she can. We haven't had a TV night since that night when I shoved my foot so far in my mouth it made it down to my ass.

I can't believe I implied she was stupid. I grip my hair, frustration with myself coursing steadily through me like it has since that night. I know better. Emma's family has always treated her like the black sheep, talking down to her, treating her like she was less than because she didn't fit the cookie-cutter expectations they had for her. She's marched to the beat of her own drum her entire life, and it's what I've always liked about her.

When she told me about the producer, jealousy ripped through me faster than it ever has before. I got angry, and I took it out on her. If only she'd let me make it up to her, fix things between us. Then maybe we could go back to how things were. It felt like we were starting to be friends. I was home more, and we would usually spend our nights together on the couch watching crappy TV with a bowl of popcorn between us. Sometimes, she'd start humming the commercial jingles, and I'd just stare at her wondering why I never noticed her like this before. The way she brushes her hair behind her ear and licks her lips when she's pulled into whatever's happening on the TV, or how she always saves the last handful of popcorn for me, even if I can tell she wants to finish it. Or the fact that she knows I like to drink a Coke at night and always makes sure to bring one with the bowl of popcorn.

She's attentive and caring in a way I've never experienced before. I've never quite been able to let my guard down with women, not even with Anna, but Emma is breaking down my walls faster than I can build them back up again.

Or at least she was before I was a total dumbass.

I slide my hand through my hair and blow out a heavy breath. Do I even want things to go back? I was pushing the line with her. I was using the excuse of friendship, but really I wanted her.

Fuck, I *still* want her.

She may not be talking to me much, but she's still walking around in her sexy little outfits. Some aren't even supposed to be sexy—they're pretty modest actually—but fuck, does she inspire my imagination in them.

I pace around my room, knowing I need to get downstairs if I'm going to try and catch her before her shift today. She's hanging out with her friend Bernie again tonight, so I know she'll turn me down if I suggest a movie night, but I want to see her.

To talk to her.

To be near her.

What the fuck are you even doing?

Scrubbing my face, I make my way to the door. Fuck it. I'm

just being a good roommate. It's not like I'm making out with her or anything.

I pass her room but stop when I hear the strum of her guitar. I pause outside the door, listening carefully as she tries a chord, then pauses, then tries again, making an adjustment to the sound. It's soft, slow, and immediately makes me feel melancholy.

Placing my ear next to the door, I try to hear the words she's singing faintly.

Don't leave me hanging on this limb,
My arms outstretched,
Aching for you to take my hand.
I know it's not what you planned.

Why can't you see?
Don't you realize you were meant for me?
My other half.
My perfect match.

Don't make me fall alone.
All I ever wanted was to call you my home.
But I can't keep choosing you
When you never choose me.
All loving you ever taught me was pain.

My heart beats hard against my chest, aching at the pain in her voice. Someone hurt her. Deeply from the sounds of it. I pull my head back and stare at her door, jealousy and anger curling in my belly.

I want his name. I want to hurt him the way he's so clearly hurt her. Emma's been hurt enough already by those who were supposed to love her unconditionally. More than anything, I can't help wishing the song was about me—not the pain part, but that she felt that strongly for me, like she'd never let me go.

A protective instinct that has nothing to do with who her brother is flares up inside me. I gently open her door and peek my head in. Her warm and open eyes meet mine and instantly shutter, causing that persistent ache in my chest to get a little more intense.

"That was really good."

Her cheeks pink up instantly, and she drops her eyes back to her guitar. "You weren't supposed to hear it," she says quietly.

I know I shouldn't ask, but I can't stop myself. I have to know. "Who's it about?"

Her gaze snaps up to mine, searching my eyes for something. I'd give it to her if I knew what she was looking for.

Once again, helplessness curls around me, making my chest feel panicky and my skin tight. I need to do something. She continues to sit there, staring at me.

"He broke your heart."

It's not a question. Her song already told the truth.

She nibbles the inside of her lip, and her eyes get glossy with unshed tears. "Yeah," she whispers hoarsely. "He always does. You'd think I'd learn by now."

My heart drops. What the fuck does she mean by that? She's still seeing this guy? Drew never said anything about her having a boyfriend.

"I didn't realize you were seeing someone." My voice sounds hollow even to my own ears.

She continues to study me. "I'm not."

Now I'm confused. "I don't understand."

She shakes her head, finally looking away, and I can't help but feel like I just failed some unspoken test.

"It doesn't matter anymore. I'm moving on."

Relief at her words courses through me. "I think that's a good idea. Clearly, this guy doesn't deserve you."

She stares at me again, giving me a look I can't read. "Yeah. I guess you're right."

She drops her gaze, almost like she can't look at me anymore. My gaze caresses every inch of her face, wishing with everything I have that I could know what she is thinking right this second. I want to see that warmth in her eyes, hear the soft tinkling of her laugh, feel the gentle touch when her fingers would accidentally brush mine when we both grabbed for popcorn at the same time.

I want back what we had. If it's all I can ever have with her, it could be enough. But this cold, closed off Emma is killing me.

I need to start by getting us back on neutral footing. "Have you had breakfast? I was going to make some bacon and eggs."

"I'm not hungry." She sets the guitar delicately in its case. "Besides, Bernie's on her way here."

Deflated, I answer, "Oh."

"We're going out after our shift, so don't wait up for me."

She grabs her purse, picks up her guitar case, and walks by me, straightening her body so that we never touch as she passes.

When I hear the front door close downstairs, it feels like the metaphorical door on our friendship, or whatever it was that had been starting, has closed as well.

THIRTEEN

Emma

Bernie's car idles at the curb, and I've never been so grateful for such perfect timing. If I had to stay in that room with Luke any longer, I would've caved and told him the song was about him. It's a little ironic he got all protective of me, saying this guy didn't deserve me when *he's* the guy.

I wonder how long it'll be before he reports back to Drew and I get a phone call from my brother asking who the guy is that broke my heart.

"How excited are you for tonight?" Bernie's question pulls me from my thoughts.

I place my guitar in the backseat and then sit in the passenger seat. "I'm a little nervous."

"Girl, you have nothing to be nervous about. You're going to blow his pants off." She shoots me a wink suggesting she thinks I should do that in the literal sense.

Tonight, I'm playing for Jason at his studio here in LA. He got back from New York a few days ago and asked me to meet him tonight. With all the songs I've been writing the past few weeks, I decided to go for it. I've been bleeding on the page—might as well share it with someone.

After I told Bernie what happened with Luke when he found out about Jason, she's been pushing me to hook up with Jason. According to her, the best way to get over someone is to get under someone else. I'm not so sure. Plus, as attractive as Jason is, I never mix business with pleasure, and I have no intention of sleeping my way onto the charts. She knows this, but she still thinks I should ask Jason out after I sing for him.

We get to work, and I busy myself with tasks, trying not to dwell on Luke, Jason, or the fact I'm about to have the most important meeting of my career so far. Halfway through our shift, I walk into the back to find Bernie bent over the office garbage can, and the smell of vomit nearly overwhelms me. Theo Walker, the owner of the restaurant, comes into the office right behind me with a glass of ice water in his hand.

He places it on the desk next to the trash and then kneels down next to Bernie. "How're you feeling?"

She just shakes her head and places her hand in front of her mouth like she's trying to stop more vomit from coming out.

Concern swirls inside me. "What's going on?"

Theo glances up at me. "Seems like Bernie has a case of food poisoning or something else that's upsetting her stomach."

He looks at her carefully. I notice his hand twitch at his side, like he wants to offer her more comfort than just bringing her a glass of water.

"Do you need a ride home?" he asks.

Bernie eases herself into the chair and rests her head in her hands, taking a few deep breaths. She shakes her head slowly and mumbles no, and then places one hand back over her mouth like that will keep her from throwing up again. When she finally looks at me, her normally olive complexion is pale, and sweat lingers on her forehead. Her usually bright eyes are vacant and wet with tears from throwing up.

"JJ's coming to get me. He's taking an Uber so he can drive

my car home." She leans her head in her hands again, as if holding her head up is beyond exhausting. "I'm so sorry, hun, but I don't think I'll be able to go with you tonight."

"Don't even worry about it. Just focus on trying to keep fluids down and feeling better."

I mean the words, but dread fills my gut at the thought of going alone. I can't help thinking about Luke's concerns over Jason. But I either risk the opportunity of a lifetime or keep my appointment and just go by myself. I may not get this chance again. I have to take it.

JJ arrives shortly after and takes Bernie home. She looks worse by the time he arrives, and I'm glad she's going to get a chance to rest, but I hate that she feels so awful. I take over her workload, and the rest of my shift passes quickly.

Before I know it, my shift is over. I change out of my uniform and into the spare outfit I packed in my large purse and then get an Uber. Nerves swim endlessly in my stomach the entire ride to the studio. When my ride pulls up outside the gate I saw on Google Maps, I hesitate to get out of the car.

Trepidation fills my gut. This doesn't feel right. I can't put my finger on why it doesn't—maybe because nothing about today has gone like I planned—but something feels wrong about this. I look out the window and bite my lip, not sure what to do. I really wish I wasn't here alone.

"Is there a problem?" my driver asks. There's a hint of annoyance in his voice, but I can tell he's trying to keep things professional, probably so I won't give him a shitty review.

"No."

Despite my instincts telling me to go home, I get out of the car, pulling my guitar case out after me. The car drives away as soon as the back door shuts, and I stare after it, unable to shake the feeling I should be going with it.

I turn back to the house. I've come this far, so I might as well go inside. I push aside any worry and head toward the gate. There's a button on the side, which I press and wait, looking around. The sun is just starting to set which only adds to my unease. I expect a voice to come through the speaker attached to the button, but instead the gate opens almost right away. Walking through, I set my shoulders back, making my posture appear strong and confident, even if I'm feeling anything but right now.

I notice Jason standing at the front door, a wide smile on his face. He's wearing jeans that are fitted in the butt and thighs and a little looser down his legs, and a black long-sleeved Henley with the sleeves pushed up his muscled forearms. Bernie would be drooling over him already, but it's Luke's face this morning that flashes unbidden through my mind.

"You look gorgeous, Emma."

His lidded gaze slides down my body, feeling just on the edge of smarmy instead of sexy. I shake off the feeling and mentally blame Luke for my unease. He's made me second-guess all this with his judgment from the other night.

Everything is fine.

Plastering a smile on my face, I reach Jason and offer him a brief hug. His hand lingers a little lower on my back than is professional, and his breath smells faintly of alcohol, but again, I brush it off. When I pull away from the hug, his hand still lingers on my back as he guides me in the house. The sound of the door closing sends apprehension down my spine.

A small voice in the back of my mind says this isn't Luke's fault I'm feeling uneasy. Something's off. But again, I try to ignore it and blame my unease on nerves.

Jason guides me farther into his immaculate house, pointing out objects here and there that he seems to be proud of. I grew up around wealth, and this screams new money. Someone trying to show off how rich they are by buying the most outrageous things. My skin crawls when he shows me a tiger skin rug, and bile rises in my throat. Isn't that illegal?

I glance around the room he guides me to and notice a small glass table off to the side where a credit card sits near white residue.

My heart beats a little faster, and I look at Jason's face, taking in the light sheen of sweat and wondering if he's been using drugs and not just the alcohol I smelled on his breath when I got here.

My gut is telling me to leave right now, but my stubbornness and determination to prove Luke wrong keeps me here.

"Do you want a drink?" he asks.

No, I definitely don't want my inhibitions lowered. "I'm good."

"You sure?" The way he asks me makes me absolutely certain I don't want a drink from him.

"I'm sure." I need to get us focused on why I'm here. "I'd love to jump right in and play some more of my songs for you. I've written a bunch of new stuff the past few weeks."

Jason's blue eyes stare at me, hawk-like. It's unnerving, but I don't fidget and refuse to give away how uncomfortable I am. I set back my shoulders and meet his gaze. Whatever he sees makes his eyes light up, which only unnerves me more.

What did he see?

What did I give away?

"All work and no play, huh?" He shakes his head, his lips quirked in a smirk as he glides his thumb across his lips. "Alright, let's head to the studio."

We walk down a hallway, several awards displayed on the walls, platinum and gold albums hanging everywhere. I recognize the name of a very popular pop artist whose first single skyrocketed her to the top of the charts. I look at Jason's back. I knew he was a popular producer from my research, but it's different seeing his success hanging on the walls.

He's the big time, and while I'm still a little nervous, I'm feeling slightly better at the reminder that he's the real deal.

He shows me through a door, and relief courses through me when I see the setup for an in-home recording studio.

God, I was being paranoid for nothing.

Fucking Luke.

My shoulders drop down. I hadn't even realized I'd been holding them so tensely until I saw the room and realized I was being ridiculous. Of course, he would have a private studio in his house. This is LA after all.

He fiddles with some dials on the sound board and gestures for me to go in the room where a mic stand and a stool are already set up. "Go on in. I'll finish getting set up out here."

"Sounds great."

I walk in, and butterflies flutter around my stomach in excitement. This is everything I've ever dreamed of. The chance to work with a big-time producer and get my music out there for the world.

He fiddles with some dials on his sound board and then speaks into the mic, "I'm ready when you are."

I pull my guitar from its case, my fingers sliding along the strings and the brand-new neck. As annoyed as I am at Luke, I'm still incredibly grateful he was able to fix my guitar.

I strum a few chords and warm up my vocal cords. "Okay, I'm ready."

He gives me a thumbs-up, and I start playing the song I was fine-tuning this morning. I close my eyes, getting lost in the song, Luke's piercing hazel eyes invading my thoughts as I sing about loving him.

Jason's voice interrupts after my second verse, and I open my eyes to see him frowning at the board. He looks back up. "Okay, try again."

I start strumming my guitar, but as soon as I open my mouth Jason stops me. "Have you ever played this with an electric guitar?"

I shake my head.

"I think it could really enhance this song. Give it a little punch."

I frown but reluctantly nod in agreement. It's not how I envisioned the song, but he's a world-renowned producer, so he knows what he's doing.

He smiles that slightly smarmy smile again. "Great. I've got one for you to use."

He comes into the studio, pushes against one of the wall panels, and it pops open to display several instruments. As I place my guitar in its case, I look around the small room and wonder how many of these panels are actually storage closets. Jason pulls out a white electric guitar with a deep red strap and walks over to me. I duck my head when he slides the strap over my head instead of letting me do it. His knuckles graze the insides of my breasts as he readjusts the strap across my chest. I cautiously glance up at him to gauge his expression, but before I have a chance, he turns away and plugs the cord into the amp and then walks back into the booth.

"Okay, try that."

I take a deep breath, trying to calm my fraying nerves, and strum the guitar. The sound that comes out throws me off. I pause and glance at him in the booth.

"Is there a problem?" he asks, his brow arched.

I shake my head and readjust the strap of the guitar. "Sorry. It's just not what I'm used to. I'll try again."

He smiles like he did the first time we met, which puts me more at ease. I start playing the song and make it almost to the end before he tells me to stop.

A frown mars his face, and he twists his lips. "You know what, I think your instincts were right. An acoustic guitar is a better sound."

Relief floods through me. I agree. I wasn't liking the sound of the electric guitar at all.

"Go ahead and switch out."

I quickly pull the strap of the electric guitar over my head and gently lean it against the wall, facing away from the window that divides the two rooms. I'm bending over about to pick up my guitar when I feel him behind me. I pop up but don't get a chance to turn around before his hands grip my hips almost painfully. He whispers in my ear, his front now plastered against my back and my heart racing so fast I'm sure he can feel it. "I can totally picture this gorgeous ass on an album cover."

My heart stops and drops to my stomach. His hand glides across my stomach, and I'm frozen in fear and shock at what's happening. "Do you know how tempting you looked all bent over and displayed for me?"

His other hand still grips my hip so tightly I know there will be bruises there tomorrow. The hand gliding over my stomach slides up until it reaches my breast and then he grips painfully.

He's whispering in my ear, but I can only hear bits and pieces over the pounding of my pulse as I remain frozen, unsure what to do. He's blocking the door, and even if I could get out of this room, he would probably catch up with me before I made it to the front door.

Not to mention, I don't even have my car here.

A tear slides down my cheek. Not only should I have listened to Luke, I should've listened to my gut when I first got here. But what good does that realization do me now?

Jason's warm breath slides across my throat, and his tongue darts out and licks up my cheek. A sob works its way up my throat, but I hold it there and pinch my eyes closed as more tears start streaming down my face.

"This is how the game is played, pretty girl. I can make you famous. Make all your dreams come true."

I feel the ridge of his erection against my back and let out a whimper, terror overwhelming me as he kisses my neck from behind me, his grip still holding me captive.

You hear stories all the time of this happening to women, especially in this industry, but it's never supposed to happen to you. You convince yourself you'll never be in that position.

Until you are.

My whole body shakes as his hand continues to rove over my body, touching me until I feel dirty and tainted.

I always thought I would be a fighter. I have enough of a temper. But here I stand, my fight-or-flight response abandoning me and leaving me frozen like a deer caught in headlights waiting to be run over.

I can't breathe. I can't think. I can't hear, except for the pounding of my heart as it races terrified in my chest.

His hand slides down to the button on my pants, and my eyes flash open.

No.

I attempt to turn around, but the hand on my hip tightens even more. "Uh-uh-uh. If you want me to produce your music, I'm going to need something from you, and I think you know exactly what I want."

He kisses my neck, and bile rises up my throat.

"No." It comes out weak.

"Don't you want to be famous?"

"Not like this." There's a little more strength this time.

"You don't mean that. Let me teach you a little lesson. I'm

the one with the keys to your future, and without me you're no one. This is how it's done, baby." I *hate* the term baby, and now hearing it from his smarmy mouth makes me hate it even more.

"No," I say again stronger, even though my tears clearly give away my fear and panic.

"Do you know who you're saying no to?" Anger seeps into his tone as his hands rove more aggressively over my body. "I can blacklist you in this town. Trust me, you want to be on my good side." He slides his hand over my pants until it rubs between my legs, and I cry harder. "Last chance at a life-changing career. Yes or no?"

Is he actually bothering to ask for consent with his hand already rubbing between my legs? Is this how he justifies his actions to himself?

"No." It comes out as a sob, but I can't help it. I'm beyond scared, and I wish I had listened to my gut when I first got here.

Jason pulls his hand away and shoves me hard against the wall, cold air instantly cooling my back. "Then get the fuck out of my house, you goddamn cock tease." His words are sharp and angry. I turn around just in time to see him walking out the door into the other room and out into the hall. I drop to my knees and take a breath, another sob ripping through my throat.

I don't think. I just move, adrenaline and survival instincts kicking in. I close my guitar case and quickly exit the room, looking for Jason around every corner, but I don't see him. I run to the front door as soon as it's in sight and leave the house without looking back. When I get onto the street, I pull out my phone and stare at it.

Who do I call?

There's only one person I want. Only one person who will make me feel safe.

Without a second thought, I find the number in my contacts list and hit the call button.

As soon as I hear his voice through the line, I let out another sob, this time in relief.

"Luke, I need you."

FOURTEEN

Luke

My heart races as I speed through the Hollywood Hills going way faster than I should, but I'm determined to get to Emma. She didn't tell me anything on the phone except where she was, but I can still hear her sobs ringing in my ears. I wanted to keep her on the line until I got to her, but her battery was dying, so she texted me the address and hung up.

I pull around the bend, searching the house numbers. As soon as I see her leaning against a wall, her head down and shoulders hunched as she holds the top of her guitar case, relief floods through me.

She's okay.

But then I notice her shoulders shaking and realize she's still sobbing. I pull over and get out of the car as soon as I put it in park. Rushing over to her, I wrap my arms around her and hold her close, feeling Emma's body sag into mine, her tears already soaking my shirt.

I pull back just enough to run my hands over her hair and my thumbs across her wet blotchy cheeks, brushing away her tears.

"Emma," I breathe out, "what the fuck is going on?" My voice shakes from the worry that's consumed me since I got her call.

She takes a shuddering breath, trying to calm herself enough to say, "I should've listened to you."

My heart falls to my stomach, and I look at the house behind her and her guitar now lying next to her.

The fucking producer.

She took the meeting with the producer.

I look back down at her, my voice low. "What the fuck did he do to you?" It's practically a growl, and I can already feel rage brewing in my gut.

I swear to God, if he laid a hand on her, I'll rip it off his fucking body.

She shakes her head and grips my arm tightly. "Please, Luke, just take me home. Please," she pleads.

Rage still coils in my gut, growing and ready to explode, but my need to take care of her overwhelms my need to murder this fucking scumbag on her behalf.

I slide my thumb across her cheek again, seeing her red and puffy eyes and wanting desperately to make this better. I grab her hand and bend down to pick up her guitar. I usher her to my car and, once she's settled inside, put the guitar in the back and get back in the driver's seat, taking her home.

Safe, where she belongs.

She's silent the whole way home. My hands grip the steering wheel until my knuckles turn white and my fingers grow stiff. I continue to glance at her as she sits in the passenger seat, silent tears streaming down her face, while she nibbles on her bottom lip.

Helplessness like I've never felt before rushes through me. I don't know how to fix this. I don't know how to make her pain go away. It doesn't help that she hasn't told me what he did. My mind is spiraling with all the ways he could've hurt her.

I desperately want to fix this for her. I'll give her whatever she needs. I'll be her shoulder to cry on, hell, her punching bag if she needs to hit someone after whatever this guy did to her.

I'll be anything for her.

She's still quiet as we pull up to my house, but her tears have stopped. The second we walk through the front door, she heads for the stairs. I stop her, holding her hand gently in mine and cupping her cheek. She stares at my chest, her hands at her sides and her shoulders drooped.

I can't take it anymore. I have to know.

The words are like broken glass coming up my throat. "Did he...did he touch you?" I ask hoarsely. It's not the full extent of what I'm worried he did to her, but I don't know if I can actually say the word.

She closes her eyes, and a tear slides down her pale cheek, which doesn't make me feel any better. I tip her chin up with my fingers, silently begging her to look at me so I can see her beautiful green eyes and the truth she usually reveals with them.

"Emma. I need to know," I beg.

Another tear slips down her cheek as she opens her eyes. "He didn't rape me," she whispers, her voice catching on the same word I didn't have the guts to say out loud.

But the truth hangs heavy in the air.

He didn't rape her, but he did assault her in some way. Just not in any way we'd be able to prove. It would be her word against his.

Motherfucker.

How many other women has he done this to?

"What do you need?" I ask.

"A shower," she whispers.

I nod and reluctantly let her go. Her emerald gaze locks on me. I slide my hand through her hair gently, and she immediately wraps her arms around me in a tight hug before pulling away and going up the stairs.

I watch her until she's out of sight, my heart aching to follow her.

Instead, I head to the kitchen to make her something I know she'll love, something comforting and familiar. Emma's always doing small things to take care of me. This is my chance to do something for her. By the time everything is ready, I find her sitting on her bed, her wet hair hanging loosely around her shoulders.

"I made you some hot chocolate," I say, setting down the oversized mug with hot chocolate and whipped cream. It's her favorite, and something I knew would offer her a little bit of comfort. I watch her take a sip, her gaze staring off in the distance.

I stand beside her bed as the seconds tick by. The same helplessness I felt in the car creeps in until I'm completely at a loss for what to do here. Should I stay? Should I go?

Does she even want me in here with her, or would she rather be alone?

I don't want to force my presence on her. Making up my mind, I start to head toward the door, but her hand shoots out and grips my wrist, stopping me in my tracks.

I look down at her, her eyes fierce and pleading. "Don't go, please."

I shake my head and sit down on the edge of the bed. "I'll stay as long as you want me."

She nibbles her lip and looks down at her bedspread before looking back at me. She whispers softly, "Will you hold me?"

Unable to speak because I'm dying to hold her, I immediately slide up until my back is leaning against the headboard and pull her gently into my arms. She comes willingly and snuggles against my side, her head resting on my chest.

For the first time since I got her phone call, peace fills me. I hold her close until exhaustion overwhelms me, and I finally drift off to sleep knowing she's safe in my arms.

FIFTEEN

Emma

Warmth seeps through my body as the soft morning light peeks through the gap in the curtains. Luke's heavy arm rests over my stomach holding me against his hard body, my back to his front. My eyes drift shut, and a smile fills my face as I let out a contented sigh. A part of me was worried I'd be alone when I woke up. That Luke would've remembered I was Drew's little sister and fled as soon as I was asleep.

I don't know what it means that he's still here, but I'm grateful he is.

Yesterday feels like a distant memory—like it happened to someone else—now that I'm wrapped in the safety of Luke's arms. Instead of wondering how long this side of Luke will last, I decide to simply bask in his warmth and comfort and cuddle with him. His breathing changes, and I know he's awake, so I roll over to see his sleepy hazel eyes watching me carefully. He keeps one arm wrapped around me, but his fingers find their way into my hair, running through it in a soothing gesture.

"Will you tell me what happened?" he asks softly.

I take a deep breath and try to process the events from

yesterday. Finally, I look at him and admit, "I should've listened to you."

He doesn't say a word, just lets me unload on him.

I tell him about how I originally planned to have Bernie come with me until she got sick and how I made the choice to keep the appointment instead of trying to reschedule because I didn't want to miss out on what could've been the chance of a lifetime. "But it didn't feel right when I got there. I should've listened to my gut, but I was stubborn."

"I think he'd been drinking," I say, looking down at his chest and replaying every moment like a movie reel. "And maybe doing drugs. There was some white residue on a table in his living room, but I don't know if it was recent. He smelled faintly of alcohol, but not overwhelmingly so."

Luke's fingers curl up in a fist, and his body becomes noticeably more tense. But he still doesn't say anything, and I'm thankful he's letting me get it all out. I'm afraid of what it'll do to me if I don't.

"We went to his studio." I roll my eyes in frustration as tears already start to fall. "I was actually relieved to see he really had one and thought I'd been silly to think the setup was sketchy." The tears fall silently down my cheeks. "I let my guard down," I say faintly.

"He came up behind me, grabbed me, and I froze. I just stood there. I just fucking *stood* there," I repeat, my teeth clenched as my frustration morphs to anger at myself for not doing more. Not fighting him or running the hell out of there. I just stood there like a damn deer in headlights. "His hands moved over my body, and I just stood there."

My gaze clashes with Luke's, and my hoarse voice cracks when I whisper, "Why did I just stand there?"

He shakes his head, clearly unable to speak.

"I have a temper. I've fought with Drew, hell, even my

parents, plenty of times, but with Jason," I say his name with disgust, "I couldn't. Fucking. Move. I stood there and let him touch me." A shiver wracks my body as I relive the moment.

I look up at Luke. "All I could think about was how I should've listened to you."

He shakes his head. "Em...," his voice breaks and the helplessness he feels is unmistakable.

"I never should've been there. He only wanted to help me with my career if I gave him my body in return." A hiccup escapes as I try to calm my breathing while fear consumes me. Luke pulls me close to him and whispers soothing words in my hair that barely penetrate the memories I'm now trapped in. When the fear finally subsides, I continue quietly.

"He ultimately gave me a choice, and I said no."

Luke interrupts me. "Forcing himself on you isn't giving you a choice." Anger is thick in his voice, but the hand caressing my hair remains gentle and soothing.

"You're right, but it could've been so much worse. When I said no again,"—I don't tell Luke I said no many times, since he's mad enough as it is and I'm worried he'll actually try to go after Jason—"he called me a cock tease and then stormed out. He said he was going to blacklist me."

I huff out a laugh, but there's no humor in it. "I actually think he does have the power to do that. Do you know who he is?"

Luke's brow furrows, and he shakes his head.

"Jason Berker. He's super famous. He's made the career of most of the pop artists on the charts right now. He's music's golden boy. And it turns out he's also a total sleaze."

I look at him, worry in my eyes, finally voicing the thought that ran through my head on repeat all night long once I was finally in the safety of Luke's house and arms. "How many other women do you think he's done that to? How many of those chart-topping pop artists were assaulted by him?" My voice cracks as more tears gather in my eyes.

Luke pulls me closer to him and hugs me tight. I wrap my arm around his middle and snuggle into him, absorbing his warmth, scent, and comfort.

"You're safe. He'll never touch you again. I promise," he says, his voice so strong and sure, he makes me believe it. I've never felt safer than being wrapped in his arms.

"What if he really does ruin my career before it's ever had a chance to start?"

"He won't."

"How do you know?" I ask.

"Because I won't let him." I hear the determination and promise in his tone, so I don't question him further. Instead, I snuggle deeper into his embrace and close my eyes, until my body finally relaxes, and sleep takes me.

An hour later, my alarm goes off letting me know I need to start getting ready for work.

"You don't have to go, you know. You can call in sick."

I nestle against his chest, wishing I could stay here all day but also knowing that I need to go to work. I need things to be normal, so I'm not just lying here all day thinking about how much worse last night could've turned out. "I need to do this. I need it to be a normal day."

Luke drops a tender kiss to my forehead that makes my heart ache with longing. God, how I wish he would treat me this way because he wanted to and not just because he feels bad for me. But I'm selfish and needy for his comfort, so I'll take it all the same. After a few more minutes, I reluctantly climb out of bed and get in the shower while Luke goes down to make us breakfast.

When I come downstairs, the table is set with coffee, eggs, bacon, and fruit. We move around each other with more ease than we have in weeks—maybe ever. When I head toward the door to leave, Luke grabs my hand and pulls me into his arms, giving me a hug that lasts much longer than is appropriate between friends.

I'm definitely not complaining.

The urge to kiss him goodbye is strong, but I refuse to make my middle school dream come true right before I have to rush out the door so I'm not late for work.

Besides, if I ever get the chance to kiss Luke Carter, I plan to savor his mouth for hours.

The day passes in a blur, my body and mind torn between moments of fear as I relive my encounter with Jason last night and bliss as I remember waking up with Luke's arms wrapped around me. I force the truth out of my mouth when Bernie, who's thankfully feeling much better, asks me what happened with Jason. It isn't until she goes on a rant about how he sexually assaulted me and should rot in prison that it really truly hits me.

I was sexually assaulted.

It still feels like a dream—a nightmare—that happened to someone else. Like an out-of-body experience.

But throughout the day, memories from last night hit me. When bending to clear a table, I remember the feel of Jason's hand crawling over my body, unwanted, while I stood frozen in fear. I can practically feel his slimy hands roaming over my body.

Later, I bump into a table and instantly feel the bruise from his fingers on my hip, which sends a wave of nausea through me.

The only thing that seems to help get me through these moments is remembering everything that happened after. Luke coming when I called. Him caring for me, his tender touch and soothing voice. Being wrapped in the safety of his arms.

Worry starts to creep in as I make my way home. Will I be greeted by the Luke I left this morning? *My* Luke?

Or will I be greeted by Drew's Luke? The guy just doing a solid for his best friend.

My heart aches a little at the thought.

I park the car in the driveway and shore up my defenses, prepared for the worst. My heart beats faster and faster the closer I get to the door, to the point where I stop right outside and close my eyes, inhaling a deep lungful of air in an effort to slow my heart rate.

I will survive, no matter what.

This wouldn't be the first time Luke's cracked my heart.

Okay, time to get in there.

I open the door and step inside, immediately hearing the ding of the microwave and inhaling the smell of fresh popcorn. Luke peeks around the corner and offers me a dazzling smile that lights up his whole face and leaves me breathless.

"Hey, perfect timing. I just cued up that movie you talked about a while back and made some popcorn. Movie night sound good to you?"

Tears burn against my eyelids, but I refuse to be the crazy girl who cries at the drop of a hat right now.

I clear my throat. "Sounds perfect."

We snuggle on the couch, his arm wrapped around my shoulders and the bowl of popcorn sitting in my lap. I glance up at him when he laughs at the movie, mesmerized that this is really happening. Luke freaking Carter is holding me.

His arm never moves away, not the entire time the movie plays. When it ends, he stands up, puts the bowl on the coffee table, and then holds his hand out to me to help me off the couch. We walk together upstairs, and when we reach my door, I feel panic seize me.

I don't want this night to end.

I don't want this perfect bubble of bliss we've found ourselves in to pop.

But I also don't want him to reject me.

I grab my door handle and then turn to him. Finding as much courage as I can muster, I grab his hand and whisper, "Will you hold me while I sleep again?"

His gaze softens, and his lips quirk up in the smallest semblance of a smile. He brushes a lock of hair behind my ear and then leans down and places a delicate kiss against my forehead.

My eyes close at the feel of his lips and warm breath against my skin. The tender gesture makes me fall for him even more.

"Sure," he breathes.

My heart soars, and I smile at him, pulling him gently into the room behind me and knowing that something has definitely shifted between us.

Now, all I can hope is that it stays this way.

SIXTEEN

Luke

The sound of the snap rushes through my ears, and I move immediately toward the ball. The grips on my gloves make contact as I take the handoff and run like my life depends on it down the field. A linebacker comes straight for me, and as he dives toward my stomach to take me down, I shift my direction. My body barely slides by him before I push myself forward as fast as my legs can carry me. Wind whips past me, but I barely notice it, the screams from the crowd washing over me and encouraging me further. When I pass the line marking the end zone, I throw the ball down and fist my hands at my side screaming, adrenaline pumping furiously through my body. I raise my arms at the crowd, and they go wild.

My cheeks hurt from the force of my smile, and my body feels lighter than air as I soak in the praise from our fans. I live for this moment.

Of course, I'm also on a high that's all Emma. We've fallen into a routine in the past week. We both go about our day—her working or playing music and me either at practice or dealing with other football responsibilities—then come home and snuggle on the couch while we watch movies we find interesting or funny TV shows. But my favorite part of the night—the part I can barely admit to myself—is when Emma asks me to hold her. Every night for a week, I've fallen asleep holding her in my arms, breathing in her lilac scent as we both drift off after a long day.

I've never been so intimate with a woman without actually getting intimate. I never touch her apart from wrapping my arm around her shoulder while we watch TV or holding her close when we sleep. I never take advantage of the trust she's placed in me. No wandering hands while she sleeps or pushing for anything. Just holding her is enough. It's left me revitalized in a way I've never experienced before.

In fact, my life would be fucking perfect if it weren't for Drew hanging over my head like a storm cloud. Despite how perfectly Emma fits in my arms—like she was always supposed to be there—it still feels like a massive betrayal to Drew. He doesn't know about her assault. She begged me not to tell him, saying he'd just end up on a flight down here and would then need bail money after dealing with Jason. She's not wrong. Drew would definitely react the same way I wanted to. He's protective of the people he loves, which adds another layer of guilt when I remember how he protected me once upon a time and all that I owe him for that sacrifice.

I reluctantly let go of the idea that I could take down the shitty producer, after I made a call to my attorney asking for his advice. He said without any evidence it would become a he-said-she-said and wouldn't result in anything. It was disappointing to hear but also not surprising. I can only hope karma hits him like a son of a bitch someday.

Since I can't destroy the man who hurt her, I've thrown myself into caring for Emma every chance I get and showing her she's protected and safe.

I thought it would be harder to be her friend. I've never

been friends with a woman before, and I never expected it to be so easy or feel like this. It could be enough just being her friend.

Probably.

Maybe.

Except you're not supposed to get boners for your friends, right? That's probably a big red flag in the friendship arena.

"Nice touchdown, man!" A hard slap to the back snaps me back into the moment. Matt gives me a high five and we run off to the sidelines, letting the defense do their thing. I'm on fire the rest of the game, scoring another touchdown before the game is over.

My victory high is still in full effect when I come home and find Emma asleep on the couch. I try to tamp down the adrenaline still pumping fiercely through me, but the sight of Emma just ramps up everything I'm feeling.

God, she's beautiful. I sometimes wonder if she realizes how beautiful she is, inside and out. She dresses confident and acts confident, but there are moments I'll catch a look in her eye, something that tells me she's maybe not one hundred percent there yet. I'd give anything to be able to tell her she's beautiful, but I feel like that definitely crosses the friendship line.

And I cannot, under any circumstances, cross that line.

I grab a throw blanket from the hall closet and drape it carefully over her body. Her face is slack and her expression serene. This might be the most peaceful I've ever seen her. My fingers itch to touch her, and before I'm even fully aware of it, my hand reaches out and gently brushes a strand of hair that had fallen across her face.

She lets out a soft hum that causes my heart to beat faster. Part of me wants her to wake up and be in this moment with me, to tell me I'm not crazy for wanting her. But the other part—the bigger part—doesn't want her to know I ever gave in to the temptation to touch her. It would be cruel to tease her with the taste of something that can never happen.

It would be cruel to tease us both.

With one more longing stare, I back away from the couch, turn off the TV, and head to the fridge to grab a bottle of water and some food. Not surprisingly, leftovers with a small bright blue Post-it note with my name on it sit on the shelf at eye level as soon as I open the door. A smile spreads across my face. She does this for me all the time, and yet I'm always somehow mildly surprised when I see it. It's just another small way that Emma takes care of those around her, those she cares about.

She cares about me.

The thought shouldn't hit me as hard as it does. I've known for years that she had a crush on me growing up. Does she still? Am I being cruel by being her friend?

My stomach sinks. I don't want to hurt her. God, that's the last fucking thing I want to do. Maybe I can't be friends with Emma. Maybe that would be pushing things too far. It might give her hope that something can happen when she has to know nothing ever can. My loyalty is with Drew. It has to be with Drew. He's been my friend and my lifeline my entire life. Hell, he's the reason I even have all that I have.

I close the fridge, leaving the leftovers in their place. I've lost my appetite anyway. It shouldn't hit me this hard. I've always known I couldn't have her. Since the first moment this spark of attraction flared to life, I've known.

Then why do I feel so gutted that she can never truly be mine?

SEVENTEEN

Emma

The bold neon flyer mocks me as I stir some cinnamon into my latte. Bernie bounces over to me—actually bounces with all the excitement of Tigger from *Winnie the Pooh*—to see what's captured my attention.

"An open mic night? You should do it."

I look away. "I don't know."

Truth is, my confidence has been shaken since the incident with Jason. And "incident" is all I'm willing to call it. I try not to think about it at all, but whenever I play my guitar or try to work on a song lately, the hairs on the back of my neck stand up like my body is bracing for attack. It usually goes away after I've played a couple of chords, but sometimes it doesn't. Sometimes the feeling lingers long after I've put my guitar away. In those cases, only Luke's comforting embrace has been able to drive the demons away.

Which has been another layer of torture in and of itself.

I thought being friends with Luke would be a step toward finally getting him to see me as a woman and not just Drew's little sister, but all it's done is put me in the damn friend zone. Except it's this weird torturous friend zone with blurred lines.

Because no matter how much I try to keep my hopes in check, I can't help thinking that friends don't usually snuggle on the couch every night like we do, or sleep wrapped in each other's arms. That doesn't feel only friendly at all. It feels like so much more, even though I know it's not.

With a sigh, I focus back on my coffee, stirring the swirling liquid even though the cinnamon is already mixed in well enough.

"Why wouldn't you take this amazing opportunity that fate has literally put right in front of your face?" Bernie asks, dramatically gesturing to the flyer.

"I just don't think my music is ready yet."

Bernie steps back, places her hand on her hip, and arches her brow. "Bullshit."

I stare at her in shock. "Excuse me?"

"You heard me. I said bullshit. You're scared."

"I am not."

"Prove it." Her high-and-mighty brow arch morphs into a challenging expression.

Damn it. There's only one way to prove I'm not scared, even though I'm actually terrified.

With another sigh, I pull out my cellphone and dial the number on the flyer. After a brief conversation with the organizer, I'm all signed up for my first open mic night in LA.

Forget butterflies in my stomach. I have a damn stampede of elephants. I don't know if I can do this. I've never been so nervous to perform, but now I feel like I might puke. My palms are clammy, and my legs won't stop bouncing restlessly under the table.

It doesn't help that Bernie keeps glancing up at the door behind me every time it opens like she's expecting someone.

"Is JJ coming?" I ask her, not bothering to look behind me again. I kept looking back whenever she would look over my shoulder, but it started hurting my neck, and that's the last thing I need tonight.

"No. He's working tonight." She sits up a little taller, and her lips quirk at the corners like she's fighting a smile.

Confused, I frown. "Then who are you waiting for?"

"Hey, did I miss it?" I turn around instantly at the voice I could pick out in a crowd.

"Luke," I say breathlessly, standing up from our table in the corner. "What are you doing here?"

I can't believe he's here.

He nods his head at Bernie still sitting at our table behind me. "Bernie told me about it." He looks back at me with a piercing stare. "I wouldn't miss this for the world."

I swear my heart's going to beat right out of my chest. He came for *me*.

"You haven't gone on yet, have you?"

I shake my head. "No, but I should be soon. I'm on deck next."

He reaches out and gently squeezes my bicep. "Then I'm gonna grab a drink from the bar. Be back in a sec."

"Okay," I say as he walks away. I plop down in my seat still staring at his retreating back.

"Do you like your surprise?"

I shake myself out of my shock fog and turn to Bernie. "How did you do it?"

"I texted him from your phone while you were getting ready for tonight. I had planned to just tell him in person, but he wasn't home. I was glad it wasn't a game night and he could actually make it."

"Thank you," I say, meaning it sincerely. I should probably be more nervous that he's here, but somehow just knowing he came for me has eased all my worries and fears. I'm suddenly excited to get on stage and show him what I can do. Show him that I'm not the same awkward girl I was when we were kids.

Okay, maybe I'm still a little awkward.

Bernie gives me a warm smile and reaches out to squeeze my hand. "Anytime, hun."

The emcee for the night announces the next performer. Only one more to go before it's my turn. Luke joins us with his beer before I have to go onstage, and when the emcee calls my name, he squeezes my hand in solidarity.

Walking confidently onto the stage with my guitar, I step up to the mic stand and ground myself in this moment. My feet plant firmly on the floor, and I feel the energy of the space move through my body, bringing me to life like a live wire. It moves from the scuffed wooden stage to my feet, up through my legs, swirls in my belly before shooting up into my chest and down my arms. With one more breath, I feel the energy rise from my chest up through my throat and out of my mouth as I strum the first chord and let my voice carry across the room.

EIGHTEEN

Luke

She's breathtaking.

I can't look away from the stage. She radiates happiness and light and all the things I think of when I think *Emma*. She's incredible, and I'm completely in awe of her.

Her voice is smooth like warm honey but filled with the same burst of energy I get right before I reach the end zone. It makes me feel alive but calmed at the same time. She brings the words to life with all the emotion her body can carry. Her fingers slide over the smooth strings of her guitar with such precision that even if I didn't live with her, I'd know she practices for hours every day.

Her voice and her guitar hold the audience captive until the final note fades away. Before she can even take a breath, I'm on my feet clapping hard and cheering for her as loud as I can.

Bernie laughs behind me, and a couple of people look at me like I'm a crazy stalker fan, but I couldn't give two shits about them. Emma just fucking rocked it up there, and I'm damn proud of her.

She walks off the stage and down the two stairs on the side. Her face is lit up like the damn Fourth of July, her green eyes bright with excitement and her smile wide with joy. She's radiant, and I want nothing more than to bask in her warmth.

It takes everything in me not to kiss her when she gets back to the table. Instead, I wrap my arms around her in a tight hug and drop a kiss to the top of her head. It's all I can allow myself.

Bernie pops up beside us, and Emma breaks away from our hug to give one to her friend. My arms feel cold, and I try to push down the empty feeling in my chest at the loss of contact.

She's just a friend. She's just a friend. You don't give lingering hugs to women who are *just friends*. Maybe the more times I say it, the more my body will get the message.

Bernie gushes about how great Emma did, and I chime in telling her how amazing she was. Pink blooms across the apple of her cheeks, and my dick pulses in my pants when she nibbles on her deep red lip.

"Thanks, you guys. It means a lot that you were both here." Emma focuses on me. "Especially you, since I know you probably had a million other things to do tonight."

"I already told you there's nowhere else I'd rather be."

She stares at me, her mouth slightly parted and her eyes looking at me with a tinge of wonder and hope. My heart starts to speed up the longer I stare at her, but I can't make my eyes break away from hers.

She lets out a shaky exhale and blinks like she just woke up from a trance. She ducks her head as if embarrassed and then turns to Bernie and starts engaging her in conversation.

I attempt to pay attention to what they're talking about, but the words go in one ear and right out the other. All I can do is stare at Emma's mouth, her ruby-red lips calling to me. I shift in my chair and discreetly adjust myself before I make an excuse of needing to use the bathroom.

There's only one other guy inside when I enter the men's room, but he quickly zips his pants and leaves—of course, not before he gives me a look like he recognizes me but can't quite place where from. I pace the length of the bathroom, internally chewing myself out and trying to get my shit together. My fingers pull through my hair in frustration.

Why does it have to be Emma that makes me feel like this? I mean, Jesus Christ, who in the universe did I piss off to make me feel all of these freaking feelings for my best fucking friend's sister?

I need to get my head on straight and figure this out. I need to put up clear boundaries for us and help Emma find an apartment. Maybe if she's not living with me, it'll be easier to ignore what she's brought to life inside me.

With my resolve set firmly in place, I exit the bathroom and head back to the table. When I approach, Emma turns around, and her face lights up again when she sees me. My heart stutters in my chest, and I know without a doubt that it's too late. The pep talk I just gave myself in the bathroom was completely useless because even if I know nothing can ever happen, it doesn't change the fact that I want it to.

I want Emma.

And now I'm going to have to fight like hell to make sure I don't slip up and make her mine.

NINETEEN

Emma

Shaking my head, I pull the blanket up to my chin, my eyes glued to the TV. "What a bunch of dumbasses. Everyone knows the killer strikes when you all split up."

I don't know what I was thinking watching a horror movie.

Actually, yes, I do. I was trying to challenge myself by doing something I've never done before—watch a horror movie from start to finish. My few friends in school used to love horror movies, but I could never stomach them. One time my freshman roommate in college watched *When a Stranger Calls* with a group of girlfriends, came home, told me the whole story line, and we both ended up having nightmares.

Yep, I had nightmares about a horror movie just from hearing the plot.

My imagination can be a scary place sometimes.

Now that I'm older I thought I could handle it.

I was wrong.

My heart starts racing as the music escalates, and I consider getting up to turn on the light so that I don't completely obliterate my future sleep with nightmares. But then the blonde girl on the screen captures my attention, and I'm frozen in place.

She turns a corner, looking behind her and breathing heavy after running from the unseen killer. The camera faces forward, and the killer grabs her at the same time that bright lights blind me and a scream rips from my throat.

"Jesus Christ, Em! Blow out my fucking ear drums." Luke covers his ears and squints at me curled up on the couch, blanket wrapped tight around me and a bowl of untouched popcorn sitting on the coffee table. He glances at the screen at the same time I find the remote and hit pause.

"What are you watching?" When he sees what's on the TV, shocked hazel eyes meet mine. "Are you seriously attempting to watch a horror movie? By yourself?"

I shrug and mumble, "Maybe."

He shakes his head and covers his mouth. It only takes me a second to realize he's trying to hide his laughter, and I chuck one of the throw pillows at him.

He catches it swiftly and offers me a teasing grin. "Come on, Em. You've never been able to watch horror movies. Why start now?"

"I made a promise to myself when I moved to LA that I was going to try new things, push myself out of my comfort zone. I thought I could handle it." I whisper the last part quietly, hating to admit defeat.

Luke gives me a tender smile and then saunters over to the couch while taking off his jacket. He slings it across the arm of the couch and then sits down right beside me, his thigh touching mine.

Heat floods my cheeks at the connection. God, what I'd give to have him touch every part of my body. To caress my skin like he desired me the way I've always desired him.

I stare at the screen waiting for him to say or do something. I can feel him staring at me, but I'm afraid if I turn toward him while we're this close, I might actually lean over and kiss him.

His body shifts and then his arm crosses my body, sliding casually across my belly. The touch warms my face further, and sirens go off in my head telling me to calm the hell down. This can't mean what I want it to.

"W-what are you doing?" I stammer.

His warm breath glides across my cheek. "I'm grabbing the remote, unless you just want to sit here and watch a paused screen for the rest of the night." His voice is husky in my ear and sends longing straight to my core.

I can't speak or breathe. I can barely even think anything apart from *Luke's arm is touching my stomach.*

Okay, so it's not the intimate touch I've dreamed about, but it's a whole hell of a lot more than the brush of his arm at breakfast or the touch of his leg pressing against mine when he sat down on the couch.

This is purposeful.

Especially when he slowly slides his arm back, the remote gripped firmly in his palm, while my nerve endings fire everywhere his arm grazes.

I bite my lip to contain the moan I'm barely holding back. Unbidden by me, my eyes stray from the TV screen and look toward him, instantly finding his hazel gaze. I have to be dreaming because I'd swear his eyes are filled with lust.

"You ready?"

I try to shake away the dirty thoughts spinning through my mind of all the ways I could ravish him on this couch. "What?"

"To watch the movie? I'll watch it with you if you're that set on trying to get through it."

I swallow forcefully and nod, afraid if I speak, I might ask him to do something else with me. Even if I wasn't imagining his heated gaze, I know he'd never act on it.

Luke presses play on the remote, and immediately another scream escapes the girl on TV as the killer attacks her. I clutch the blanket to my chest and try to focus on the movie, but my senses are hyper aware of everywhere Luke's leg touches mine, his steady breathing, and the occasional glances he casts my way.

I finally get absorbed in what's happening on the screen and sit frozen, blood rushing through my ears and my heart pounding so furiously I'm sure even Luke can feel it because it has to be shaking my body as I wait for the next horrifying moment. Suddenly, the killer strikes out of nowhere, and a scream escapes my throat. Instinctively, I curl toward Luke and bury my face in his chest, my heart racing and my body shaking uncontrollably.

Why, oh why, am I such a wimp?

Embarrassment floods me at the chuckle that escapes Luke's chest. I glance up to see mirth skirt across his face before his hand comes up to brush aside a lock of hair from my cheek. Our eyes meet and everything stops. I can't hear the movie over the whooshing in my ears from my pounding heart. But this time it's not pounding in fear.

His lips are *right there*. I glance at them before looking back into his eyes and see his pupils dilate and his breathing stall before coming out heavier than before. I lick my lips and watch in fascination as his eyes drop to them, and that heated look I thought I was imagining before comes back tenfold.

We both lean forward until our lips are just a breath from each other. The ax murderer from the movie could jump out of the screen and I'd be none the wiser because all I can focus on are Luke's perfect lips and how close they're coming to mine.

"Luke," I whisper, longing clear as day in my voice.

His eyes snap to mine, losing their lusty drowsiness and immediately filling with guilt. My heart drops into my stomach at the change that comes over him.

"We can't, Emma. *I* can't. Drew would never forgive me."

He clears his throat and jumps up from the couch. "I, uh, I forgot I need to watch some game tape to prep for tomorrow. So, I'm gonna go do that. You should, uh, probably just skip the horror movie. They're overrated anyway."

"Yeah, sure," I say, the movie the last thing on my mind while my heart cracks at his rejection.

He's just about to exit the room when I call out to him, "I made too much dinner, so I put the leftovers in the fridge for you."

That's a lie. I made extra so he wouldn't have to cook after a long day and grueling practice, but like hell I'll admit that to him now.

He grips the back of his neck, an apology written across his face. "Okay. Thanks."

He walks out of the room, and I find the remote to turn off the movie while I try to fight back tears.

But what did I honestly expect?

Did I really think Luke would actually make a move? It's a small relief that at least I know I haven't been imagining his attraction. For once, I'm not alone in my feelings.

I'm just alone in wanting them to turn into something more than just distant longing.

TWENTY

Luke

I'm in trouble.

Big fucking trouble.

I'm falling for my best friend's little sister.

In my defense, she's too fucking loveable for her own good.

She's sweet, smart, sassy, and downright sexy. Her laugh has made me hard more than once in the past week. The way she moves, talks, sings, dances around the kitchen while she's waiting for the coffee to brew—all of it is driving me crazy with an insane need to claim her as mine. I want to ravage her and bury myself so deep inside her I won't know where I end and she begins.

It's a goddamn miracle I've lasted this long without kissing her gorgeous, luscious mouth. I almost lost control of myself the other night when I attempted to watch that horror movie with her. She was just so...perfect. After weeks of falling for her, noticing all the ways she silently takes care of me—cooking for me, leaving encouraging Post-it notes all over the house on game days, and even setting up my favorite movie in an attempt to cheer me up when I came home from an epic loss—I nearly caved. She was *right there*, her lips a breath from mine, her eyes screaming at me to claim her. And fuck did I want to claim her.

But I caught myself at the last minute. I already know there will be no going back if I kiss her. I'm too far gone already. So, I've been trying to get us back into the friend zone.

But Jesus Christ, she's really pushing all my restraint.

Especially when she cuddles on the couch with me in her skimpy pajamas that have me so distracted, I couldn't even tell you what movies we've watched this week.

Or when she grazes her body against mine when she walks past me in the kitchen while I'm cooking breakfast or dinner and sets my skin on fire.

Or when she laughs at my stupid jokes, and her whole face lights up with joy.

And definitely when she snuggles against me before falling asleep, and I feel like I'm finally breathing for the first damn time in my entire life.

My phone rings, pulling me from my spiraling thoughts, and I glance down at the caller ID to see it's my mom.

"Hey, Mom."

"Hey, baby boy," she says, using her favorite term of endearment.

"What's up?"

She starts talking about what's going on at her country club, and I half listen, knowing she doesn't expect me to respond. I love my mom, but she's a pretty self-centered person. Her comfort and happiness always took priority when I was growing up. I often wondered why she even bothered to have a kid. I don't doubt she loves me. She just loves herself more.

"Luke? Did you hear me?"

"Hmm?" I ask, realizing she changed topics when I wasn't paying attention.

"I talked to your dad. He said he's been trying to reach you."

Instantly, my mood darkens. "Mom, seriously, this again? Why do you care? You two aren't even together anymore. Why do you even still talk to him?"

"Luke, you know we are still in the same social circles. We can be cordial, and it's important to keep up appearances. Why aren't you speaking to him?"

I close my eyes and pinch the bridge of my nose, already wishing I hadn't answered the phone. "Mom, it doesn't concern you."

"Sweetie, I know your dad can be difficult, but he's the only dad you've got. You'll regret it if you don't fix this."

Anger spikes in my gut. "What makes you think I'm the one who needs to fix this?"

"Well, your dad is clearly trying to reach out to you, so he's done his part. Now you need to do yours."

Clenching my jaw, I grind out, "Mom, you need to let this go."

"Luke—" she starts, but I instantly cut her off.

"Enough, Mom. I'm not talking to him. It's okay for you to leave him, but I can't?"

"That's not fair. Did you want me to be miserable? You know how unhappy we were together."

Oh yes, I'm well aware of how unhappy they were. The constant yelling, condescending comments that were perfectly designed to cut each other down, and then when they finally did divorce, their attempts at using me to get back at each other. It's one of the factors that drove me to spend as much time at Drew's house as I could get away with.

"So you get to leave when you're unhappy with him, but I can't?"

"It's not the same thing, and you know it."

"How is it any different? He made you miserable, so you left him. He makes me miserable, so I don't talk to him anymore. Seems pretty similar to me."

"He's your father."

"So? You act like that means something. Just because we share the same DNA doesn't mean I owe him anything. Is this why you called me? To try to guilt me into talking to him? Why does it matter to you?"

"I just don't want you to look back at this and regret it."

"If I do end up regretting it, at least I'll be regretting *my* choice and not someone else's. Let this go, Mom, or it won't just be Dad's calls I'm screening."

Silence reigns on the other end before I hear a small sniffle. My shoulders sag, and I roll my eyes, preparing myself for the guilt trip I set myself up for. Before my mom has a chance to start, my phone beeps, and I glance at the screen to see Drew is calling me.

Happy for an excuse to get off the phone with my mom, I say, "Sorry, Mom. I gotta go. I'll talk to you later."

I end the call with her and accept Drew's call. "Hey," I say, my voice still tense from my phone call with my mom.

"Uh-oh, I know that tone."

I release a heavy breath. "My mom's hassling me about not talking to my dad again."

"You wanna talk about it?"

"Not particularly. Not right now, at least," I amend. It might be helpful to talk to him about it later and get it all off my chest.

"Just let me know. How're things with Emma?"

It takes my brain a second to process his question and remind myself that he doesn't know I've slept with her in my arms every night for the past few weeks, except for the night when she fell asleep on the couch. And while all we've done is sleep, I still don't think he'd be entirely comfortable with it.

"Uh, things are good."

"She's not been too much of a burden?"

"No, she's been great. She's a hell of a lot better as a room-mate than I remember you being in college."

"Whatever, man. You weren't exactly roommate of the year, especially when I had to put up with your smelly football gear all the time." His tone turns earnest. "But in all seriousness, I can't thank you enough for what you've done for Em."

My stomach rolls with guilt.

"She attempts to do everything on her own and rarely asks for help. I blame my parents for that. They've tried so hard to push her into this specific image they had of her, so she learned early on to dig her heels in and do things her own way. Well, you know. You've been around for all of it. Anyway, she means the world to me, and I can't tell you what a weight you've lifted from my shoulders by looking out for her, especially since it's taking her a bit longer to find a new place than I expected."

I close my eyes in pain as my guilt suffocates me. If he only knew the thoughts that swirl through my head about her on a daily basis. If he only knew how close I've been to sacrificing our friendship just to taste her lips.

"No problem," I choke out, unable to say much more.

He continues on, and the longer he speaks, the more my resolve grows. I can't let this go any further with Emma.

Scratch that. I need to pull way the hell back and bury these feelings that have emerged. I can't betray Drew. Not after all we've been through together. And definitely not after what he did for me in college. I can't forget that I owe him for everything I have.

"Shoot, I just noticed the time. I gotta head to court. I'll talk to you later," Drew says, immediately ending the call. I put my phone in my jogging band and lock up before setting out for my run at a decent pace. Thoughts swirl in my head as I push my body forward.

I need to stay away from Emma.

I need to just be her friend. Except maybe less of a friend than I'm currently being since that also feels like crossing a line.

The problem is I don't want to.

I want to kiss her hair when we're lying on the couch watching movies.

I want to take her out in public and hold her hand, showing the world she's mine.

I want to taste her—every fucking inch of her gorgeous, freckled, porcelain skin.

My fingers run through my hair in frustration while I push my body another mile, my headphones blaring Linkin Park as I try—and fail—to drown out my conflicted thoughts.

How do you choose between the friend who's always had your back and the one woman who's made you want *more*?

After a few miles, I round the corner and slow my pace as I reach my house. I know Emma will be awake once I get in there, and I don't know if I'm ready to see her.

If I'm ready to—once again—deny all that I'm feeling.

God, I hate feelings.

I'm angry at Drew for even putting me in this situation in the first place. I never would've fallen for her if she didn't live with me.

So, really, this is all his fault.

Fuck, that argument is weak. Now, I'm just grasping for anyone to blame but myself for the situation I've found myself in.

I approach my house, my gut tied in knots and this feeling of helplessness overwhelming me. I've never felt like this. I've never hesitated to go after what I want. But what I want now is in direct conflict with the one friendship I've valued above all others.

Bending over and stretching my hamstrings, I inhale deep

and release the tension in my body, stuffing all my worries and concerns deep down in the box where I bury all the other feelings I'm not ready to process.

When I stand back up, my shoulders release the tension they've been holding, and my chest doesn't feel so tight.

Everything will work out.

It has to.

But then the minute I get inside my house and see Emma standing at the stove, all my conviction to stay away from her disappears.

TWENTY-ONE

Emma

Luke wasn't in bed with me this morning, and I felt his absence like a two-ton weight.

I keep waiting for him to pull away from me entirely, and I can't help but wonder if today will be the day I've been dreading.

The day where he'll finally put distance between us.

I'm not so naïve as to believe that Luke would ever really choose me over Drew. Whatever we've been doing the last few weeks most likely comes from his concern for me after my ordeal with Jason.

Now if only my heart would get that memo.

Unfortunately, the heart wants what the heart wants. And my heart has always wanted Luke.

Stupid thing.

I trudge down the stairs, my whole body heavy with the disappointment coursing through my veins. I get the coffee started, hoping that'll be a good pick-me-up, but not even the divine smell of coffee brewing can pull me out of my slump.

When the front door opens, my whole body tightens, preparing for the gentle letdown I know is coming.

I wrap my emotions around me like a shield, feeling the stirring of tears but refusing to let them fall. Wanting to be distracted and busy when Luke comes in the kitchen, I get to work on making breakfast. The squeak of his running shoes on the tile hits my ears at the same time that my body becomes painfully aware of his presence behind me.

"What are you making?" Luke asks as he walks around me toward my fresh brewed coffee and grabs a mug from the cabinet above the coffee maker.

"Cheesy eggs and hash browns." I don't tell him potatoes are my comfort food, and I was about to eat my feelings in breakfast food.

Glancing in my periphery, I watch as he leans his butt against the counter and crosses his legs, his arms crossed over his sculpted chest and his empty coffee mug in his hand.

I don't look at his eyes, but I can feel the weight of them on me.

"Do you want some?" I ask quietly.

"That'd be great."

Silence, apart from the sizzling of the hash browns as they cook, fills the kitchen.

My gaze is focused on our breakfast, but the rest of me is completely attuned to every movement and sound coming from where Luke is standing.

He clears his throat, but I still don't look at him, afraid if I do, he'll see everything I'm thinking and feeling.

"You okay?" he asks softly.

"Yep," I say, slightly popping the p. I reach into the cupboard and grab the Johnny's seasoning I packed from home. This stuff is amazing on everything. There's no way I was moving to LA without my own stash.

"You sure?" My ears pick up the hint of concern, and I

finally look over at him. His hazel gaze is locked on me, and his body is stiff.

"I'm fine." I'm used to saying that to my family, but the words leave a nasty taste in my mouth giving the lie to Luke.

His expression tells me he doesn't buy it. His eyes slide back and forth between mine, and he chews the inside of his lip before speaking again. "I have practice today, but I'd like to take you somewhere tonight. Are you free?"

Is he asking me on a date?

I stare at him, the crease between my brows deepening slightly while I try to figure out what's happening. I thought he was going to let me down easy, but now I'm wondering if I read the situation wrong.

Or jumped to conclusions—which certainly wouldn't be the first time.

"I'm free," I reply, my heart thundering in my chest at the possibility of this being a date.

The tightness around his eyes softens slightly as his lips curve up in a subtle smile.

"Great." He walks over to me and drops a kiss on my forehead that has me practically melting to the floor while my heart soars out of my body. He drops his forehead to mine, and his voice is husky when he says, "I'm gonna run up and shower before breakfast is finished."

I can't speak. He's so close. If I just tipped my head up, our lips would meet.

God, what I would give for him to kiss me.

His hand comes up and gently cups my face, his thumb grazing the apple of my cheek. My breath stutters in my chest while my heart beats at a dangerously rapid pace.

My gaze slides up his throat, over his parted lips, until it locks on his gorgeous hazel eyes that are filled with so much heat, it steals whatever breath was left in my chest.

Kiss me.

I beg the words silently, convinced my gaze is screaming my desire for him. His stare drops down to my mouth, and I inhale sharply when he licks his lips. His gaze shoots back up to mine, and dread seeps into my blood at the conflict in his face.

What would it take for him to choose me?

He swallows and steps away, leaving my body cold and wanting.

Clearing his throat, he says, "I'll be back down in a few."

"Okay," I say quietly, but he's already racing up the stairs.

Away from me.

I turn back to the stove, my brain trying to process everything that's going on between us. Things have changed, but I still don't know if he'll let himself truly feel what I can see in his eyes.

Would he ever take a chance to be with me?

Or am I not worth the risk?

I chew my lip and fight back the familiar hurt that comes with wanting someone so desperately and knowing he'll never really be mine.

Because deep in my bones, I know without a doubt, Luke will never choose me over Drew.

TWENTY-TWO

Luke

I'm hoping my plans tonight put Emma and me on better footing than when I left the house this morning.

Things were awkward when I came back down from my shower.

I'd been so close to kissing her before my brain finally caught up to my body and screamed *abort!*

The line is getting so blurred I'm not sure I even know where it is anymore. I want her more than I should, given how much her brother means to me. But every time we're together, the only thing I can think about is kissing her, claiming her, making her mine.

I don't even see Drew anymore when I look at her.

I know tonight is crossing the boundary even more, but I'm also pretty sure she'll love it, and it's the thought of her eyes lighting up in pure happiness that pushes Drew completely from my mind.

I shower and change at the training facility after practice and then head straight home. Nervous energy thrums through me, my hands tapping on the steering wheel and my left leg bouncing the entire drive home.

I pull up to the house, park in the driveway, and then walk to the front door, shaking out my arms in the process and hoping to dispel some of this anxiousness before I see Emma.

Fuck, I hope she likes what I have planned.

When I walk into the house, I immediately pick up the lyrical sound of her voice from the living room and the strum of her guitar as she covers a song I heard on the radio the other day. As much as I liked the radio version, I love hers. Her voice soothes every piece of my soul until I'm standing at the edge of the living room completely enraptured by her.

She glances up right as she hits the last line, her gaze locking on mine through the final notes.

It isn't until she stops completely that I realize I wasn't breathing.

I clear my throat, feigning the confidence I'm usually known for that has completely abandoned me. "Hey."

Hey? Really, dude?

God, this woman has me so twisted up I can't even come up with a good opening line. I feel like I'm seventeen again.

"Hey," she responds, watching me carefully.

"You ready to go?"

"Where are we going?" She's curious, but there's something else in her tone too. Something I can't quite name but has me wondering if I tie her up in knots as much as she ties me up.

"It's a surprise."

She stands up, turns around, and places her guitar in its case on the couch before facing me again. "Am I dressed okay for what we're doing?"

My gaze slides down her deep red hair falling in luscious waves over her shoulders, the ends just barely reaching her plush breasts. She's wearing a purple off-the-shoulder dress that wraps around her curves but flares out right above her knees. I remember an ex-girlfriend calling a dress like this a mermaid style. Whatever it is, it's peak fifties pinup and has me salivating for a taste of her.

I clear my throat, not as capable of exuding confidence this time, and respond truthfully. "You're perfect."

A blush stains her fair porcelain cheeks, and my fingers twitch with the desire to touch her, but I hold back.

I should call this night off. I'm on the precipice of doing something I can't take back. Of choosing her when I know I shouldn't.

When I know my loyalties should lie with her brother.

But...I don't think I can hold myself back any longer.

She steps closer, her lidded eyes raking over me in my dark denim jeans and black button-down long-sleeved shirt.

Yeah, I dressed up.

Even though I haven't put a label on it—and I don't intend to—a big part of me wants this to be a date.

For just one night, I want to pretend like I'm not her brother's best friend. Like she's just some woman I met and fell for.

A woman I could actually let myself have and consider a future with.

Instead of doing the smart thing and calling this night off, I open the front door and gesture after her. I walk her to my car and hold open her door. Then I rush back in the house and grab her guitar. She'll be bummed if she doesn't have it for this.

She gives me a curious look when I carefully place her guitar case in the back seat, but she doesn't ask me why I'm bringing it, and I don't offer her any explanations. I hand her the black satin blindfold I bought for her, knowing she'd figure out my plans as soon as she saw where we were going and wanting the surprise to linger as long as possible.

"Here."

She stares at it, but her hands remain in her lap. "What's that?"

"It's a blindfold. I want it to be a surprise."

Her gaze slides up to mine, but she remains quiet and takes the blindfold, securing it around her head.

Pleasure thrums through me at the trust she's placing in me.

The drive is mostly quiet, apart from the alternative music playing softly from my stereo. I catch Emma humming along and smile to myself. When I glance over, my heart beats a little faster at how beautiful she looks with the fading light of the sun making her skin glow.

I have to turn back to the road, knowing if I continue to stare at her, I'll never want to stop. My chest feels tight and heavy, like there's a pressure in there that's unfamiliar but not necessarily unwelcome.

By the time we get close to our destination, I'm so worked up, my body is sparking like a live wire. I really hope she likes this. I've never cared so much about impressing a woman, but I care now.

I care with *this* woman. I want her to be impressed with me.

It's in this moment, I know it's too late for me. I want her. I want her more than I've ever wanted any woman. She's everything I never knew I needed, and I know that not even my friendship with Drew will stop me now. I'm too far gone.

I drive a little farther and then park at our destination. I guide her through the entrance until we're standing at the heart of the stage, her guitar case securely in my other hand. Then I move just in front of her and to the side so I can watch her reaction.

"Okay, take off the blindfold."

She slides the black satin from her face and blinks, her eyes adjusting to the bright lights. She looks around and then inhales sharply as soon as she realizes where we are.

She turns to me, her eyes wide. "The Hollywood Bowl?"

I nod, clenching my jaw and waiting to hear if she likes it or not.

She looks around again, her eyes roving over every inch from where she stands in the middle of the stage. When she turns back to me, her eyes are watery, but she has the brightest smile on her face outshining the lights around us.

She looks fucking breathtaking, and it no longer feels like I'm standing on the edge of a precipice, but that I'm in the freefall before I meet the ground.

TWENTY-THREE

Emma

My gaze locks on his, unshed tears filling my eyes as my heart soars.

I can't believe he did this. It's been my dream since I was a little girl to sing on a stage like the Hollywood Bowl. And he made it happen.

I don't even care if there's no audience.

He's here.

He did this for me.

"Luke..." Words die on my tongue because I'm speechless. Hope fills my heart more than it ever has before.

"Play something," he says, his voice hoarse and low, his eyes locked on me and filled with warmth and something I'm afraid to name because my hopes are already through the roof.

Unpacking my guitar, I pull the strap over my head and adjust my hold. I look back over the empty seats and the bright lights, then close my eyes and strum the chord of the newest song I've been working on.

My voice carries swiftly across the bowl, the acoustics heaven to my ears. The song starts slow, but then picks up until

I'm belting the chorus, pouring all the emotions stirring in me into the song.

The one thing I've always loved most about music is the ability to tell the truth. To put whatever you're feeling into words and be completely exposed. It's like you're cutting yourself open for the world to see, but you're still protected by the cover of the music.

I can stand here and spill my heart—my hidden truths about a man I love who's standing five feet away from me—and not feel scared because he has no idea it's about him.

I strum my guitar, letting the final note fade in the air before opening my eyes, my lashes damp from tears I hadn't even realized I'd let loose.

Pride and incandescent happiness fill every ounce of my being. I'm on the best kind of high. I turn my head to find Luke staring at me, conflict and pain in his eyes, and the smile falls from my face.

"Was it bad?" I ask, my throat already tightening at the idea he hated it. I absently slide my guitar around my back so I can cross my arms in front of me in some lame attempt to protect myself.

He shakes his head and clenches his jaw before scrubbing his hands over his face. I watch him closely, trying to figure out what's going on. He seemed fine before I started singing.

It has to be the song.

My heart drops.

Did he figure out it was about him?

"Luke—"

He cuts me off. "I can't do this anymore."

I take a shuddering breath and try to shore up my defenses, but I'm wrecked from singing my heart out only moments ago and feeling extra vulnerable.

Nibbling my lip, I say, "Okay."

He shakes his head, walking toward me. "No, Emma, not okay. I can't fucking pretend anymore. I can't stand here and watch you light up and not fucking kiss you."

My lips part on a gasp, but before I can respond, his mouth is on mine, and my mind goes completely blank as I melt into his kiss.

I've dreamed of this moment for most of my life, but the real thing is even more perfect than any dream. His mouth molds with mine like it was made just for me. His tongue licks across the seam of my lips, begging for entry, which I grant without hesitation.

He kisses me like I'm his only way to breathe. Like he'll waste away if his lips aren't on mine. I kiss him back with the same intensity and passion, pouring my heart into our kiss.

His hands come up to cup my cheeks and move my head the exact way he wants it. I moan into his mouth, butterflies soaring in my stomach and my hands gripping his hips to keep him against me.

The unmistakable firmness of his erection presses against me, and we both moan at the friction.

He breaks our kiss, leaning his forehead on mine and breathing heavily like he just ran a marathon.

I stare into his eyes, searching for answers.

What was that?

What's going through his mind right now?

What do I have to do to get him to kiss me again?

"Emma..." he whispers, and his voice is needy, but there's an underlying pain there. My heart falls and I close my eyes, waiting for the inevitable. Waiting for him to tell me this can never happen again because of Drew.

I've never resented my brother. Not when my parents constantly asked me why I couldn't be like him. Not when he brought Luke home for the first time and claimed him as his.

Not even when he struggled to understand my dreams, because in the end he always supported them.

But I'm starting to resent him now. This is the closest to pure happiness I've ever felt, like everything I've ever wanted is right at the tip of my fingers, and my stupid brother is about to take it away from me.

A tear falls silently down my cheek while I wait for Luke to speak. To dash the hopes he built up so quickly during our kiss. At least I'll always have the memory of his lips pressed against mine. It'll have to be enough.

When he still doesn't say anything, I finally open my eyes and look at him. He's staring at me, his thumb rubbing circles on my cheek.

I can't take it anymore. Pulling away, I turn from him and walk toward my guitar case. Maybe if he isn't touching me when he breaks my heart, it won't hurt as badly. "It's okay, Luke. I understand. It was a mistake. A heat of the moment thing. I won't tell Drew."

My voice doesn't break, which is a damn miracle. I wish I could say the same for my heart.

I close the latches on my case and stay squatting, giving myself an extra moment to compose myself before I have to face him again.

"Emma?"

I stand up, pushing my shoulders back, and turn back to him.

His brows are furrowed, his stare locked intently on me. "Do you really think it was a mistake?"

I chew on the inside of my lip, already hating the lie I'm preparing to spew. But he doesn't give me the chance.

"I don't."

My gaze locks on his. "What?"

He starts walking toward me, his expression determined,

but still watching me carefully, "I don't think it was a mistake. Do you?"

My eyes dart frantically between his, searching for some indication that he might be stringing me along. But I don't see anything but determination, honesty, and concern the longer I let the silence sit between us.

"No," I finally whisper.

He stands before me now, the toes of his shoes practically touching mine, our gazes never leaving each other. He brushes a lock of my hair behind my ear and lets his hand rest there, his thumb stroking the edge of my jaw. "I could never regret kissing you."

I'm afraid to speak. Am I dreaming?

But I have to ask, "What about Drew?"

The pain I saw earlier flashes in his eyes, but he blinks it away and focuses on me. "I don't want to think about Drew right now."

"What do you want?" My whole body vibrates with nerves, both terrified and excited for his answer.

He leans down, his lips a breath from mine. "You."

His lips take mine in a kiss that would bring me to my knees if he wasn't holding me up with his other hand. I don't know how long we stand there kissing each other, our mouths perfecting a dance I'm convinced they were made for, but we're both breathless when he finally pulls away.

"Let's go home."

The second the front door closes behind us, his mouth is back on mine.

I worried the whole ride home that he'd talk himself out of

this. I convinced myself he'd remember Drew is his best friend and I'm Drew's sister and Drew would kill us both.

But clearly my worries were for nothing, because his kiss is ravaging, and within moments the only thing I'm thinking about is getting him naked.

I start unbuttoning his shirt, my fingers clumsy and shaking because I'm so desperate for him. He wraps his hands around mine, halting my movements and causing my eyes to glide up his throat until I'm looking into his hazel hues.

"There's no rush, you know." There's a smile in his eyes and a teasing tone to his voice, but I still feel a desperation clawing at me like I absolutely have to rush before he changes his mind.

I've thought about this moment a million times since I hit puberty, and it's already surpassed every single one, so I can only begin to imagine how amazing sex with him will be.

So, yeah, I'm rushing.

We can go slow during round two.

As I stare up at him, I realize I have no idea how to explain how I feel. To tell him I'm like a starving lion in the wild and he's the first gazelle I've seen in months seems a little ridiculous.

Instead, I give him the truest truth. "I don't want you to change your mind."

His gaze softens, and his hands slip into my hair, holding my head so I'm forced to keep looking at him. "There's no way I'm changing my mind about this. I've been thinking about it for weeks."

"I've been thinking about it for years," I whisper, vulnerability seeping through every inch of my body.

I expect pity, but it's not what he gives me. His piercing stare gets fierce and hungry, and before I know it, his mouth is kissing me everywhere.

My lips.

My jaw.

My neck.

My chest.

He doesn't leave a single inch untouched by his lips.

When he makes it to my breasts, I slide my fingers into his hair, holding on for dear life because this is already better than any foreplay I've ever had.

I rake my nails through his hair and hold his head to my breast. He growls—actually *growls*—and then stands up tall, staring down at me, his chest heaving in time with mine.

"Fuck it. I'll go slow next time."

Yes! Finally!

A squeal leaves my lips when he sweeps me up into his arms like I weigh nothing and carries me up the stairs. I expect him to go to my room since that's where we've been sleeping, but instead he walks down the hall to his room. He puts me down and spins me around, sliding the zipper of my dress down my back until it's completely undone. His hands glide over the sleeves that already sat off the shoulder and have now slipped down to my elbows. He pushes them completely off and then kneels down and gently tugs the dress over my hips until it falls in a heap on the floor.

His breath fans my lower back as his hands caress my calves and up my thighs. He moves his hand up between my legs and slides his fingers over the sensitive bud where my thighs meet causing me to inhale sharply at the jolt of pleasure. He kisses where my thigh meets my ass cheek, and my eyes close while my head tips back and I struggle to find a breath.

My heart is beating rapidly as he continues his way back up my body, kissing and caressing me so tenderly I'm convinced if I didn't love him already, this moment would seal my fate. When he stands back up, he gently twists me around until I'm facing him and kisses me, his tongue hungry for mine. Without breaking the kiss, he gently pushes me onto the bed and continues where he left off in the hall downstairs, his mouth mapping my entire body.

By the time his mouth makes it to the apex of my thighs, I'm strung tight like one of my guitar strings. Luke looks up at me, his hooded eyes sending a rush of desire to my core. Without breaking eye contact, he slides his tongue up the seam of my lower lips, his eyes closing in bliss for only a moment before he opens them and does it again, this time sucking my clit into his mouth. My back arches off the bed, and I know if he keeps this up, I'm not going to last long.

His hazel eyes spark at my reaction, and he dives back in like he's ravenous for something only I can provide.

I have never—I repeat, *never*—had a man show such enthusiasm for oral sex, but holy shit. Within minutes, stars are flashing before my eyes as I come apart. His mouth doesn't slow, not even when I drop back to the bed, my chest heaving while I try to catch my breath.

"Again," he says, his voice a growl.

I lift my head and shake. He has to be kidding. But then my eyes close in ecstasy as he slides a finger inside, then two, hitting that place deep inside. He pumps repeatedly, and the motion combined with the sucking of my clit has me soaring again.

He kisses my thighs and then stands up and removes his shirt in record time. I watch with lidded eyes, enraptured by his six-pack and fit body from hours in the gym every day. It's his job to stay in shape, and it shows.

As soon as his hands reach for his belt, I sit up, placing my hands on top of his and looking up at him. "Let me."

He lets his hands drop to his sides and watches me as I unbuckle his belt and pull it slowly through the loops. His lips still glisten from my release, and his eyes are so dark now they almost look brown instead of hazel. I unbutton his pants, then hear the scratch of the zipper, my eyes still glued to his while my hands work to free him from the remainder of his clothes.

I finally look down when he's completely naked, and my breath stalls. Fuck me, he's got a beautiful cock.

I've never thought of a man's cock as beautiful before, but I'm salivating at the sight of it. I don't know if it's because I'm in love with him or because he's just that magnificent, but either way, I don't hesitate in wrapping my lips around the tip and sucking.

He tips his head back and groans, spurring me on. I lick his shaft and gently squeeze his balls before wrapping my lips around and taking him as far as I can. He hits the back of my throat repeatedly before I finally pull my mouth off. When I look up at him, his eyes are hooded, his lips parted, and his chest heaving.

"Don't stop," he says hoarsely as he brushes my hair away from my face.

I tip my lips up in a smile and then bob back on his cock. His fingers slide into my hair, and he moves my head at the pace he wants. Wetness floods between my legs as I submit to him and let him use my mouth for his own pleasure.

He doesn't let me suck him long before he pulls my mouth off his shaft and bends down to kiss my swollen lips.

"No more," he says, breathing heavily. "I have to be inside you."

"What are you waiting for? An invitation?"

He smirks and shakes his head. "Smartass," he mumbles while lifting me up and laying me back on the bed. He reaches over to his nightstand and pulls a condom from the drawer. Once it's on, he climbs onto the bed and settles on top of me. His cock is primed at my entrance, but he just holds himself over me, and my smile falls from my face at the seriousness of his expression.

His gaze meets mine. "There's no going back after this."

My heart aches in my chest. "Is that what you want? To go back to how things were before?"

He breaks our eye contact and rests his forehead on my chest while taking a deep breath. "No."

His voice trails off like he wants to say something else, but instead of speaking, he pushes into me. I arch my back, pushing my chest against his at the feel of him snug inside me.

Pure unadulterated bliss flows through me.

My God. This man is everything and more.

All my fantasies get blown out of the water as he rocks in and out, his pace quickening as we both get lost in the sensation.

"Fuck, you feel so good," he breathes out.

I grip his ass, pushing him into me as my hips rise to meet his thrusts. "Don't stop," I whisper.

He speeds up. "Never."

Luke slides his hand over my breast then down my stomach until his thumb is rubbing circles on my clit.

The gentle motion spirals my orgasm into an explosion of fireworks, and I scream out his name, convulsing as pleasure wracks every inch of my body. My legs shake uncontrollably around his hips as I ride out my orgasm. His thrusts increase until he's pummeling into me and shouting out my name.

I will never, for as long as I live, forget hearing Luke Carter yell out my name as he came.

He stills inside me and looks down at me, his chest glistening with sweat and his eyes slightly dazed from his release.

He slowly pulls out, both of us gasping from how sensitive we are, and then drops beside me on the bed, his arm resting over my stomach and his head leaning against mine.

I sigh contentedly and can't stop the giant smile from taking over my face. Luke's hand slides up my body until he's cupping my cheek. He turns my face toward his, amusement clear in his expression.

"I take it the smile means it was good for you too?"

A laugh bubbles up out of my chest. "I can't believe you even have to ask. Are you searching for compliments? I didn't think that was your style."

"I like to know I did a good job. That really shouldn't come as any surprise seeing as I get a high off the praise of fans on a daily basis."

"I suppose you're right."

He pulls his head back slightly, a small frown on his face. "So, you're not going to tell me you liked it?"

I smile, a little giddy at the idea I have someone as confident and sexy as Luke Carter worried that he didn't satisfy me.

What an insane idea.

I turn to him, my gaze softening as I cup his cheek with my hand. "It was more than I ever imagined."

His eyes light up with a smile as he pulls me close to him. I curl up, soaking in his warmth and his strong body holding me so tight, and fall asleep wishing the night never had to end. That we could stay in this bubble, just the two of us forever.

I should've known better.

TWENTY-FOUR

Luke

A ringing pierces the serene quiet of my room, and I blink one eye open, feeling Emma stir next to me. The whole night rushes back in a split second, and I pull her tighter to me and drop a kiss on her bare shoulder.

The ringing continues, and I turn to my nightstand to see my phone lit up, Drew's name flashing on the screen. My body tenses at the realization that he's calling me while his little sister is lying naked next to me because we spent all night having the best sex of my life.

Fuck.

"What's wrong?" Emma's voice is scratchy from sleep but alert. She must've felt me tense behind her.

"Nothing. It's your brother. I gotta take this."

I crawl out of bed and grab the phone on my way to my dresser. I need to get out of this room. I can't talk to Drew while Emma's here. In my bed.

Guilt that I betrayed my friend grips me, but I don't regret my night with Emma. Even if it's about to make my life a hell of a lot more complicated.

"Hey, man, what's up?"

"Hey, is Emma with you?"

My heart stops, and my mouth gapes open trying to figure out how to answer that. I grab a pair of boxer briefs and slide them on quickly.

"Uh, no. Why?" I ask, exiting the room and walking down the hall.

"Well, she's not answering her phone, and it's still early so I figured maybe she was still home with you. Do you know where she is? I haven't heard from her in a few days."

My eyes close in relief. And then guilt washes over me again.

"Uh, she might be with Bernie." I wince at the lie. I hate lying to Drew, especially because I know he's calling out of concern for his sister. But what am I supposed to do? Tell him, yeah, man, I know exactly where Emma is—in my bed, naked.

I don't think so.

Concern fills his voice. "You okay? You sound weird."

I sit on the top step and rest my forehead in my hand, my gaze falling to the floor. "I'm fine, dude. I just woke up, and I'm a little out of it. I'll tell Emma to call you the next time I see her."

"I'd appreciate it. I gotta go, but I'll call you later."

"Sounds good."

We hang up, and I rest my hands over my bent knees, trying to figure out how to proceed. I never foresaw this situation. I'm not a guy who fails, but I feel like I'm failing pretty hard right now. No matter which path I choose, I can't help feeling like someone is going to end up getting hurt. Staying loyal to Drew means I have to end whatever this is with Emma. After last night, I don't think I could give her up even if I tried.

I run my fingers through my disheveled hair, hoping an answer will come to mind. I just need time to figure this all out.

"Do you regret it?" Emma's quiet voice asks behind me.

I turn around and take in her bare legs, my gaze sliding up to see her body covered in only my shirt which barely covers the space between her legs that I was buried in last night.

My gaze moves all the way up until I meet her eyes, and my breath stutters in my chest at the forlorn look on her face. Like she expects me to tell her I regret being with her. My heart breaks at the pain in her eyes.

I stand up and move toward her until I'm right in front of her.

"I will never"—I bend down while lifting her chin, so she's forced to meet my gaze—"I repeat, *never* regret a single moment with you. Do you understand?"

A tear slides down her cheek, and she nibbles on her lip, her cheeks pinking up. She stares at me like she's afraid to believe me, and I can't really blame her. I've always chosen Drew. But things are different now. She's different. She's made me feel things I didn't know I could feel. I can't give her up.

"I just need time to figure all this out, okay? Let's just keep this between us for now."

The words feel like glass against my throat, like I'm making her my dirty secret. And I hate it, but I can't be seen being affectionate with her in public until I figure out how to handle telling Drew.

"Is that okay?" I stop breathing, realizing there's a very real possibility she could say no to me. I don't know what I'd do then.

She stares at me, her eyes searching mine, and finally nods her head. My shoulders sag in relief.

I just bought myself a little time.

Now I just need to figure out how to keep them both.

Matt's hand reaches out to help me up. "You okay, man? You're having a spectacularly shitty time out here tonight."

"No shit," I grumble, shaking out my limbs and knowing I'll be sore as fuck after this game. I've taken so many hits tonight, I'm starting to think my position on the field is to flatten the turf.

I'm better than this.

Or I am when my head isn't all fucked up. Anger rises up and shuts all my other emotions down. Emotions never solve anything. I need to lock that shit down so I can focus on what matters—making a plan for how not to blow up my friendship with Drew and my budding relationship with Emma.

I run to the sidelines as defense comes onto the field. Emma's face filters through my mind, and I can clearly see her flushed cheeks as I brought her to orgasm twice in the shower this morning.

Three days of fucking her on every surface of my house and I still don't feel like I've had enough. The more I have her, the more I worry I might never get enough of her. The more my need for her grows.

But it's more than sex too. It's her making coffee while I make us breakfast, and the nightly routine we still have of cuddling on the couch and watching TV. It's the quiet moments when we're lying in bed and learning more about each other. Even though I grew up with her, there's so much I never knew about her. She's brave, and strong, and fascinating. She's also gotten me to open up to her in ways I never have with a woman. I've never trusted any of them enough, but Emma makes it so easy to trust her.

I've never felt so content and fulfilled in a relationship.

If only I could figure out a way to tell Drew about us without losing him, then everything would be perfect.

"Luke?"

I turn to see Matt staring at me, his eyebrows raised. "Huh?"

"Dude, you are massively out of it today. You need to get your head in the game."

I turn back to the field, resolve firming in my gut. He's right. I do need to get my shit together.

I shove my emotions down and refocus on what matters.

The next time we're on the field, I channel all my energy into the plays and go back to being the machine I was born to be.

TWENTY-FIVE

Emma

Is four days too soon to tell someone you love them?

Well, more like a lifetime of loving someone from afar and then having them make love to you for four days straight.

That's not too soon, right?

Although, Luke was super distant when he got home from his game last night, and really it's only been four days for him since we got together.

So, yeah, definitely probably too soon.

My fingers itch for my guitar, the flicker of a song coming to life in my mind, but I'm at work and the song fades away before I even have a chance to consider running to the back room where I keep my purse during my shift. Bernie moves around me to clear the plates from the table next to mine, and then we both make our way back to the kitchen at the same time.

"Girl, whatever you're smoking, I want some."

I turn to her, confused. "What?"

"You have been flitting around here with a giant smile on your face, in the happiest mood. I think you have to be high on something...or someone." She winks.

I bite my lip and shake my head, but I can't stop the huge smile or the blush on my cheeks from breaking out on my face.

"I knew it!"

"You know nothing," I reply.

"Don't Jon Snow me right now. You got it on with that handsome roomie of yours, didn't you? Girl!! Why aren't you bragging to everyone that walks through the door?"

My smile droops a little, remembering exactly why I've been keeping quiet about our sexcapades.

Because Luke wants to keep it a secret.

Because of Drew.

The thought leaves a sour taste in my mouth.

It's the only blemish on our otherwise perfect connection. Apart from his distance last night, he's attentive, kind, caring, tender, and yet ravaging in the bedroom.

He may not be entirely perfect, but he's damn close.

And he's perfect for me.

I finally feel like things are starting to fall into place. I have the man of my dreams, and I'm working on the career of my dreams.

Pulling me from my thoughts, Bernie asks, "So, are you guys a couple now?"

I don't actually know how to answer. We're together, but we haven't had the talk about putting a label on what we're doing. Will he even want to label it while he's still trying to figure out how to tell Drew?

"I'm not sure," I tell her, dying to confide in someone. "He wants to keep it on the DL until he can figure out how to tell Drew."

"Your brother? Why don't you just tell him?"

I'd already thought about that too. "Because Luke feels it's better if he does it, and I want to give him the opportunity to tell Drew himself."

"So, when's he going to tell him?"

Good question.

I shrug, my heart aching a little as a deep insecurity bubbles up to the surface—that Luke is just going to keep me as his dirty little secret.

No. He wouldn't do that to me.

"I'm not sure."

Bernie frowns. "He's not rushing to tell your brother." It's not a question, and the look she gives me tells me she thinks that's sketchy as fuck.

"I'm sure he's going to tell him soon," I say before making my way back out to my tables, the whole time worrying that Luke might not ever be ready to tell Drew about us.

Then where would that leave us?

By the time I get home, my feet are killing me, and my head is pounding. All day long, worst-case scenarios swam through my head, feeding on every little insecurity I've ever had. I'm ready to just curl up in bed and go to sleep. I'm not even sure I want to see Luke. I'm afraid he'll be able to read all the turmoil on my face. I've managed to plaster on my customer service smile all day, but I'm exhausted and can't maintain the ruse in my own space.

A big part of me doesn't want Luke to see how much he's affecting me. How much his indecision on how to handle *us* is wreaking havoc on my confidence. I mean we haven't even been together a week!

God, I'm a mess.

Maybe I just need him to define this so I know where we're going. That at least we're going somewhere, and I'm not just a passing fling.

I round the corner and stop in my tracks when I see two place settings on the dining room table, tall red candles, and a covered basket that smells like it's hiding warm rolls inside. Luke comes out of the kitchen wearing a pair of denim jeans that sculpt his ass in the most delicious way and a tight heather gray T-shirt that shows off the tattoos going down his arms.

His oven mitt-covered hands place a casserole dish on the table and then he turns and sees me.

"Hey." His handsome face lights up with an easygoing smile as he slides off the oven mitts and walks over to me. His attitude is already a complete one-eighty to how he acted last night after his game. Maybe it didn't have anything to do with me at all. Maybe he was just in a bad mood because they lost.

"Hey," I say as he wraps his arms around my waist and pulls me close. "What's all this?" I ask, gesturing to the table behind him with lit candles.

He leans close, his lips whispering against mine. "I thought I'd make us a romantic dinner."

All the tension I've been holding throughout the day dissipates as my heart melts at his romantic gesture. A smile curves my ruby lips as I glance back over at the table.

He kisses my cheek and then nibbles my ear, causing my eyes to close in bliss. "You know, since we can't actually go out to eat at a romantic restaurant."

My eyes snap open, and my heart stutters in my chest, that achy feeling coming back strong.

"So, you did this because you can't be seen with me?"

He pulls away, his stance confident, and the only hint that he's not in control of the situation is the slight furrow of his brows. "You know we can't go out in public. Not until I figure out how to tell Drew about us."

I pull away from him and take a step toward the table, my

eyes taking in all the effort he put into this. As sweet as it is, it doesn't answer the question that's been nagging me all day.

I turn back to him. "What even is this? I mean, what are we doing here? It's been several days, and you still don't have a plan for how to approach Drew about us. I can't help but wonder if it's more that you don't want to tell him about us, because there is no *us*. Am I just a fling to you, Luke?"

He opens his mouth to speak, but I cut him off. "It's fine if that's the case. I just need to know."

He frowns and crosses his arms. "You want a label."

I look at him pleadingly, wishing he could understand how hard this whole conversation—hell, situation—is for me. "I just want to know what this is. I need to keep my expectations in check. If this is just sex to you while I live here, then I need to know so I don't expect anything else from you."

He gestures toward the table. "Does that look like just sex to you? I can't remember the last time I made dinner for a woman I was seeing."

"But you did it because you don't want to be seen in public with me."

He runs his hands through his hair, clearly exasperated with me. "It's not that I don't want to, Em, it's that we can't. I can't blindside Drew like that."

"It's never going to be easy, Luke. This whole thing is going to blindside him no matter what. We just need to tell him."

"No."

He says it so quickly and so adamantly, like there's no other possible answer.

I cross my arms over my chest and stand tall, holding my ground. We both stare at each other, neither of us saying a word. But the longer the silence drags on, the more my heart aches, and I start to feel the familiar burn of tears behind my eyes.

Emotion clogs my throat as he continues to stand there, not saying a word. Not explaining why it's such a hard no.

I can't help but wonder if that "no" is an always no. I know he said he was thinking up a solution, but the way he responded just now tells me he's not really. He's avoiding. He's hiding us here in his house.

I can't stand it anymore.

"If you're not going to tell him, then whatever this is"—I gesture between the two of us—"should stop. Clearly, it's not going anywhere."

I see his hands drop to his sides before I turn on my toes and move to the other side of the room toward his backyard. I need space from him. The tears escape the second I turn away, and I cover my mouth in an attempt to quiet my sob. I feel the heat of embarrassment on my cheeks and wish—not for the first time—that I didn't cry so easily. That I could be strong and composed in these situations instead of a bubble of emotions that always bursts when I least want it to.

"Em..." Luke says quietly behind me, pain in his voice.

I suck in a breath and control my voice as best I can. "I don't think there's anything else to say."

"Fuck that. There's plenty to say." His voice gets closer, until I feel him standing at my back. "I don't want to stop," he says softly.

Brushing the stray tears from my eyes, I move to face him, and he immediately steps forward, cupping my face and brushing away the tears I've missed with his thumbs.

"Emma. It guts me to see you cry on a normal day, but knowing I'm the one who caused these kills me."

"What are we doing, Luke?" I whisper, my eyes locking on his and searching for some kind of answer. I need to know what he wants.

His hazel gaze never leaves mine. "If you need a label, then I want you to be my girl."

My heart leaps, but my brain reminds it to settle down. There's still one more major obstacle in our way.

"And what about Drew?"

He sighs heavily and pulls me close to his body in a tight hug, leaning down and kissing the top of my head. "I need time. Drew and I have been through a lot of shit together. He's going to see this as a betrayal, and I can't stomach that right now. I just need a little time to wrap my head around all the different ways he could respond to this and figure out the best approach to get him to see us as a couple without wanting to murder me or end our friendship. I can't lose him, Em." His voice cracks, and another tear slips down my cheek as I realize how torn he's feeling.

He pulls back to look at me. "But I can't lose you either."

TWENTY-SIX

Luke

Adjusting my cufflinks, I chance a quick look at the clock. Damn. I hope Emma is ready soon or else we're going to be late to Jack and Paige's wedding.

It crushed me when I made her cry the other night. I thought I was doing a sweet gesture by making a romantic dinner at home—something I've never done before—but I should've thought about how it might come across to her. I know it might be a little risky to take her to the wedding, but the idea of going without her causes a painful knot to form in my gut. I won't be able to touch her as freely as I want to, but at least she'll be with me.

I pull out my phone and shoot a text to Matt. I know he'll be at this thing, and I'm wondering if he's there already. Before I get a response back from him, I hear Emma's steps coming down the stairs. I glance up from my phone and stop breathing at the sight before me. She's wearing a figure-hugging emerald-green dress that brings out the green of her eyes and perfectly complements the rich red of her hair, which falls in soft curls over her shoulders. My stare follows the curves of her body, and the effect she has on me is undeniable.

She's absolutely breathtaking, and I can't believe I'm the guy who gets to call her mine—even if only in private for now.

The drive is short since traffic is light. When we get to the venue, I look around at the number of people in attendance. There are probably at least two hundred folks present. I immediately see Matt, surrounded by a bevy of beautiful women, although I notice his eyes keep gazing across the room to Denton's daughter.

God, I hope he's not stupid enough to put his dick in Nikki Denton. Coach will kill him.

Emma and I make our way down the aisle to find a pair of seats. Not long after, Matt sits down next to me.

"Hey, cool if I sit here?"

"Sure," I reply.

He glances at Emma, and nods when he sees she's already looking at him. I clear my throat and offer introductions.

"Matt, this is Emma Delaney."

His eyes widen slightly, and I notice he casts his glance down to where my leg is flush against Emma's before his eyes come back up to meet mine.

His brow arches. "The roommate? Your buddy's sister?"

"Yeah, remember I told you about her."

He nods and says low so only I can hear, "You didn't mention she looked like a pinup."

The soft music changes and gets louder, signaling the start of the ceremony and cutting off my chance to respond.

It's probably for the best because I'd feel like the biggest piece of shit if I had to deny my feelings in front of Emma. We stand and all look toward the back where Paige enters, looking gorgeous as ever. A smile graces my face at how happy she looks, her eyes focused ahead of her and not seeing anyone but the man she's walking toward. I glance at the altar to see Jack, his eyes red rimmed and his jaw dropped in awe. He puts a fist in front of his mouth, clearly trying to hold himself together.

Unfamiliar emotion swirls in my chest, and a deep desire to feel what he's feeling nearly overwhelms me. I glance over at Emma to see her looking at Jack as well, a smile on her face and tears already filling her bright green eyes.

She must feel the weight of my stare because her gaze quickly shifts from watching Jack to looking at me.

I don't know what I did in my life to deserve this woman, but it's suddenly clear to me the pressure I'm under not to fuck it up. Somehow, I already know after only a week that Emma would be impossible to get over. She's nothing like any of the women I've dated in the past.

No, Emma's the kind of woman you promise forever to. The woman you spend your whole life proving you're worthy of.

Matt bumps my shoulder, and I turn to him, quickly realizing everyone else is facing forward again, now that Paige has reached Jack.

He eyes me and then Emma before taking a seat right as the minister invites us all to sit. I try to focus on the wedding, but thoughts keep invading my mind. Thoughts about what it'd be like if Emma walked down the aisle to me. The thought of her walking toward anyone else is unacceptable.

The heat of her leg burns through my pants, and the longer we sit here, the stronger my desire grows to take her hand in mine.

Instead, I look to Matt, hoping he'll say something that'll help me reset and focus on why we're all here today. When I catch his gaze glued to a blonde several rows ahead of us and on the opposite side of the aisle, I realize he's as distracted as I am.

Relief fills me for a split second that he actually seems to be interested in a woman again. He's been in a weird dry spell that is completely out of character for him. Or at least, I think he has.

I haven't seen him hook up with anyone on our away trips or talk about anyone here in LA.

But my relief soon fades when I realize his gaze is locked on Nikki.

"You're going to burn a hole in her head if you keep staring," I whisper. I drop my voice a little lower. "Not to mention what Denton will do to you if he sees you eyeing his daughter."

"Why don't you worry about your own issues," he whispers, throwing me a knowing look and glancing at Emma, who fortunately is focused on the happy couple.

I frown at him and turn back to the wedding ceremony happening in front of us, my shoulders stiff and body tense. If he can tell there's something going on between Emma and me, then there's no way Drew would miss it.

Heaviness settles heavily on my shoulders at the weight of the choices I know I need to make—and soon.

The catered dinner tastes delicious, and the reception venue looks just as enchanting as the ceremony did. I quickly discover that Emma doesn't just captivate my attention. She seems to draw everyone at our table to her, apart from Matt who's off in his own world most of dinner and then ditches us the second Coach walks out the door. I watch the dumbass head straight to Nikki like she's a beacon calling his name.

Curious about what's going on with him, I watch them closely. When I see the look on her face, I realize something's already happened between them. It's confirmed when she takes his hand and joins him on the dance floor. His face lights up as he stares intently at her. I've never seen him look at a woman like that. He holds her close to him, affection and intimacy flowing between them. I look around and see Will and Gina on the dance floor holding each other closely as well.

Turning toward Emma, I watch as Gabe Romero sits back in his chair, his head thrown back in laughter. Gabe is a total badass on the field and one of the Fierce Four—the nickname coined for our four fiercest defensive players, who have become rather infamous within the league. I shake my head in awe of Emma and how seamlessly she's fitting in with my friends and colleagues.

I lean closer to Emma. "Sorry to interrupt you two, but I'm gonna steal my date for a dance."

I stand and hold out my hand for her. Her face instantly breaks out into the largest smile, and my heart beats a little faster knowing I'm the one who put it there. She takes my hand, and I pull her out onto the dance floor, joining the other couples in pulling her close against my body.

The words of the slow song filter through the speakers, piercing my heart with how apropos they are for how I feel in this moment with Emma in my arms. But the words that hit me the deepest are when he says he'll never stop choosing her. I glance down at Emma, whose head is resting against my chest, her eyes closed and a serene smile on her face.

This moment makes it feel so easy to choose her. Apart from football, nothing has ever felt more perfect than holding Emma in my arms.

Guilt quickly seeps into my bones because even if this feels right, I know it's not. Drew trusted me with her, and he'll see this as a betrayal of that trust. No matter how I try to spin it. Drew's the only consistent family I have, even if we're not related by blood. He's always had my back.

A memory from sophomore year of college flashes through my mind, once again reminding me how much I owe Drew for all I have in my life.

And how badly I've betrayed him by hooking up with his sister when he explicitly told me not to.

"Look how in love they are."

I glance down at Emma, who's now looking over my shoulder. I move my head to see who she's looking at and see Jack and Paige, holding each other close, foreheads touching and dancing slowly, lost to each other like no one else is in the room.

I look back down at Emma and find her already staring up at me, a tender smile pulling up the edges of her deep ruby lips. "I love you, Luke."

Every inch of me freezes. My feet plant on the floor, and my breath remains frozen in my lungs, my eyes locked on Emma as her words weigh me down. My lips are sealed tight while my brain goes haywire.

I attempt to open my mouth to say...something, but it's like my jaw is glued shut. All I can do is stare at her, my eyes wide with surprise, and it kills me—fucking guts me—when I see the sadness enter her eyes at my complete and total inability to say those words back to her.

It's not that I don't care for her. In fact, I undoubtedly care about Emma more than any woman I've ever been with. I'll admit I'm definitely falling in love with her. But falling is different than being in love.

Isn't it?

"Emma...I, uh..." I look up hoping for some kind of inspiration to help me out of this grave I'm digging for myself and see Coach Denton walking toward his table. I look over at Matt and Nikki, who are dancing near us, completely enamored with each other and neither noticing the disaster about to happen.

"Shit."

Like a train wreck, I watch everything moving in slow motion as Coach reaches the table he'd been sitting at and grabs a shawl hanging off the back of a chair. His gaze slides up, and the second it lands on Nikki in Matt's arms, his face goes hard with rage. In a split second, I move Emma and me behind Matt and hiss his name.

He looks up at me, and I gesture behind him with my head at the same time that Nikki goes noticeably stiff in his arms. He glances down at her before finally turning around and catching the infuriated gaze of our coach. Nikki steps immediately out of Matt's arms, and I don't miss how his shoulders sag at the loss.

What the hell is going on with these two?

She walks over to her father and speaks to him softly, but his gaze is locked on Matt. I watch as Matt makes his way over after Nikki's father orders her to leave the venue—an order she immediately complies with.

I step closer, just enough to catch the tail end of Matt's heated but contained conversation with Coach.

He leans into Coach's space. "Nikki isn't a plaything at all. It's not like that."

Coach responds, his face red, "I'll tell you what it is—nothing! Whatever you were doing with Nikki is done. Stay away from her. If I hear that you've seen her outside of a professional capacity, then your time with the Wolves will be done. Do you understand me?"

Coach doesn't wait for a response but immediately spins around and storms out of the room. Matt watches his retreating back, his shoulders sagging even more than when Nikki pulled out of his arms on the dance floor.

"You okay?" I ask, patting him on the shoulder.

He shakes his head. "Not even close."

"What do you wanna do?"

He stares at the exit, his eyes sad, like he just lost the best thing he's ever had. I stare at him and can't help wondering if this is what I'm going to look like when shit hits the fan with Drew.

And it's definitely a when, not if, situation. I know Drew too well. Unless I've already messed everything up with Emma because I couldn't tell her I love her.

My jaw goes slack, and my heart slows. Fuck. I don't want to lose her.

I reach behind me where I can feel Emma at my back and clasp her hand in mine, needing the reassurance that she's still with me.

None of us are in the mood to stay, so Emma and I walk out with Matt to his car where we part ways—him with a promise to fill me in on what's going on with Nikki Denton sometime. Emma is quiet as we walk to my car and the whole way home. She barely even looks at me, which I can't really blame her for.

When we get home, she mumbles something about wanting to change. I let her go, watching her as she walks away from me.

Suddenly, my concern over how to tell Drew seems completely inconsequential. Instead, I'm left wondering if I just fucked everything up all by myself.

TWENTY-SEVEN

Emma

The scalding hot water pelts against my skin, but I still feel cold. Covering my face with my hands, I let out a groan. God, I'm such an idiot. I can't believe I told Luke I love him. It's been a week! No wonder he stared at me like I'd lost my mind.

I blame the wedding. I got so wrapped up in the romance of the day, seeing a couple so completely in love with each other made me realize how much I love Luke. I spent half the wedding daydreaming that it was our wedding—Luke staring at me with such love and devotion that no one could ever doubt his feelings for me. Then we were dancing, and the song was talking about how he's never going to stop loving her, and the words just popped out.

Now I'm hiding in the shower, wishing I could take them back. Not because I don't mean them, but because they've exposed me and left me vulnerable in a way I don't want to be with Luke.

I know he doesn't love me—it's been a week, come on—but a small part of me desperately wanted to hear those words come out of his mouth. I wasn't surprised when he didn't say them, but I was taken aback by how disappointed I was.

I'm also beyond embarrassed. I was almost relieved when Luke's friend Matt had some drama, since that pulled Luke's attention away from me allowing me to hide my mortification that I let my feelings slip out so freely. I was even able to avoid talking to him on the drive home. But I won't be able to hide from him much longer. We sleep together.

I shut off the water and grab my towel off the rack, holding it to my face as I try to figure out how I can diffuse the awkwardness that will inevitably be there when I'm in the same room as Luke again. I won't apologize for my feelings, because truthfully, I'm not sorry about how I feel. I'm just sorry I dumped it on him like that when it's obvious he's not there yet.

I towel off and throw on some comfy pajamas. I make my way downstairs and find him sitting on the couch staring at a glass of whiskey in his hands. He looks up when he hears me enter, and my chest gets tight. He's so incredibly handsome, his brown hair perfectly styled to make me long to run my hands through it, the scruff on his face giving him a sexy David Beckham vibe, and his piercing hazel eyes searching mine.

God, I love him so much.

Yeah, there's no hiding that. I'm suddenly lost with how to act. How do I brush it off, so he knows I'm not expecting anything from him?

He stands up and walks toward me, placing his glass down on the coffee table on his way. When he reaches me, he instantly slides his fingers through the hair at the base of my neck and around until he's gripping the back of my neck. He pulls my head up as he drops his down and places a searing kiss against my lips. My hands reach up to grip his biceps, silently begging him never to stop kissing me like this.

All too soon, he breaks the kiss and rests his forehead on mine. "Emma."

My name sounds like a prayer coming from his lips—so soft and tender.

He pulls away so he can look me in the eye. "I've never said I love you to a woman before."

My eyes go wide in shock, but before I can say anything, he continues, "You have to know, what I feel for you—it's so much more than anything I've ever felt before. I might not be able to say those words yet, but I promise you no one has ever owned me the way you do. You're all I think about. You're all I want. I hope that can be enough for now."

I'm speechless. This is more than I expected from him—even if it's still not quite what I hope for.

He bends down, imploring me with his eyes to answer him. I nod and say softly, "It's enough for now."

Relief moves swiftly through his body, and it's just now that I notice how tense his shoulders were and the strain around his eyes that's now disappeared as he smiles at me.

He scoops me up in his arms like I weigh nothing and carries me back up the stairs toward his room. "What are you doing?" I ask.

"I'm going to spend the rest of the night showing you how much you mean to me."

I smile and wrap my arms tighter around his neck. "If you must."

He won't hear any complaints from me.

The rich aroma of coffee fills the air as I move around the kitchen wearing one of Luke's Wolves T-shirts and nothing else. Women in the movies always make it look so sexy wearing their men's oversized shirts, but the reality of being a thick girl means it's snug across my large breasts and wide hips. If it was a standard T-shirt, it probably wouldn't even cover my ass, but this cut seems extra long, so it falls just below my butt cheeks.

I gracefully move toward the fridge, grab my creamer, then turn back to the coffee maker. The whisper of a song tickles my brain, but I can't grasp the rhythm or words, something I've noticed is happening more frequently these days.

Long, tattooed arms wrap seductively over my hips and then up around my waist, pulling me back against the warm, now very familiar body that I left in his bed only ten minutes ago. His mouth drops to my neck, his warm breath causing goose-bumps to break out along my skin. His tongue slides along the curve of my neck up to my ear, and my pulse pounds heavily as wetness coats my thighs.

A soft sigh escapes as he continues erotically kissing my neck, and the stiffness of his erection makes its presence known along my back. He slips his hand beneath the shirt, and his big hand slides up my body until it reaches my breast. He gives it a gentle squeeze before his thumb and forefinger pinch my nipple hard. The sharp bite of pain is quickly soothed away when he spins me around and sucks my nipple into his mouth.

I close my eyes at the sensation and grip his hair in my fingers, holding his head to my breast as his hand caresses my other breast.

"Luke." My voice comes out as a needy whimper. I thought I enjoyed sex before, but no man has ever worshipped my body the way Luke does.

He owned my heart before, but every day that I spend waking up in his bed, feeling him rock between my thighs, his cock, tongue, and fingers taking me to heights I never knew possible, the more I'm convinced he owns my body too.

Who am I kidding? He owns all of me, heart, body, and soul.

My fingernails scrape across his scalp eliciting a long groan from him. He looks up at me, his hazel eyes heated and sparking with desire before he gives me a smirk that causes a Pavlovian response in my body. Every time he looks at me like this, I know I'm about to experience an orgasm that takes me to another world.

Luke drops to his knees and drapes my leg over his shoulder before diving into my pussy like it's the only breakfast he's ever desired.

Stars blind my vision when he sucks my clit, and I come on a gasp, breath whooshing out of my lungs as my legs shake and bliss sparks across my nerve endings.

He gently kisses the inside of my thigh and then places my foot back on the floor and holds my waist as he stands up. His mouth molds over mine, his tongue sliding across my lips seeking entrance that I quickly grant. Our tongues dance against each other, the taste of myself still present on his tongue.

There's something erotic and a little naughty about tasting myself on his tongue. It sets my blood on fire and only increases my desire for him. He groans again and then lifts my body until I'm sitting on the counter's edge, his body nestled between my thighs. My hands glide across his broad bare shoulders, grateful he didn't bother with a shirt this morning.

It would only end up on the floor anyway.

I'm also grateful we had a talk about the fact that I'm on birth control, and we don't need to use condoms anymore.

My fingers slide over his pecs while our mouths duel for dominance. My hands work their way down his body until they meet the edge of his gray joggers. I push them down, and he breaks away from my mouth long enough to kick them off. His strong hands grip my lush hips and pull me closer to the edge, lining up his cock with my sex before he slides easily inside.

We both moan at the connection. No matter how much sex we have, the first time he slides into me always feels like a dream, surprising me with the heady pleasure it elicits.

One hand slides behind my neck, gripping my hair and pulling my mouth to his, while the other slides between us and rubs my clit. His hips thrust faster as the first flutters of another orgasm hit me before turning into a full-on quake. My pussy clenches around him while stars spark in my vision once more. With one more thrust, he comes with me. When the last of our tremors settle, he drops his head to my shoulder.

"I don't think I'll ever get enough of you." His words are spoken so softly, I wonder if he meant for me to hear them or not.

He pulls out of me slowly and drops a lingering kiss on my forehead. "I'm gonna go take a shower before practice."

"I'll make us some breakfast."

"Thanks, Em," he says with another quick kiss before he dashes up the stairs. I watch him go, feeling restless. My skin feels too tight, but I can't pinpoint what's making me feel this way.

Things are good with Luke—mostly. Even though he didn't say he loved me, he showed me all night long. The only other thing I can think of that would cause this is how hard it's getting lying to Drew. I've never lied to my brother and usually share all the big details of my life with him. Falling in love with his best friend definitely qualifies as a big detail, and it feels wrong that he doesn't know.

I slide off the counter and quickly clean everything up before dumping my now cold coffee down the drain and preparing a fresh cup. As the coffee machine gurgles and the aroma of fresh brewed elixir fills the air, I make a decision.

I need to talk to my brother. Soon.

TWENTY-EIGHT

Luke

The warm tap water runs over the suds as I rinse off the last plate and put it in the dishwasher. Emma sidles up beside me in a tight black tank top. My eyes scan down her delectable body, and I fight back a groan when I see the formfitting leggings that accentuate her perfect ass.

The things this woman does to my body are insane. I reach out and cop a feel of her luscious tits, causing her to squeal and slap my hand away.

"Oh my God, your hand is wet!"

I nuzzle her neck and nip at her ear before whispering, "I'm about to make you wet."

She laughs, the sound causing my heart rate to spike with an unfamiliar emotion. She turns her body into mine. "You always make me wet." Her throaty voice carries her words straight to my dick.

Groaning, I pull away because as much as I'd love to bury myself inside her again, I don't want her thinking I only want her for sex, and I feel like most of what we've done lately is have sex.

Lots and lots of mind-blowing, life-changing sex.

But she means more to me than just a physical release. A whole lot more. The reality is she means more to me than any woman ever has.

Grabbing the dish towel off the counter, I lean my hip against the counter and face her. There's a strain around her eyes and mouth that didn't used to be there, and I hate the feeling that I'm the one putting it there. All because I couldn't say I love her or even grow a pair and tell her brother that we're dating.

The hardest part is she doesn't even understand why I'm struggling so hard with this.

I clear my throat. "Emma, this situation is way more complicated than any I've ever been in before." I reach out and grab her hand, sliding my thumb over her fingers and staring down where our hands are clasped together—my large hand dwarfing her small, delicate one.

"Drew isn't just my best friend; he's practically my brother. He's been there for me through every horrible thing in my life. When my parents got divorced my freshman year of high school, when my mom got remarried to her dick husband, when my grandpa died." I pause and chew on my lip, staring off across the room at nothing in particular, not sure how to admit this to her. Drew and I swore we'd never talk about the truth with anyone.

My gaze refocuses on her, memorizing the flecks of dark green in her eyes. My voice is quiet when I confess, "Drew saved my ass in college. He's the only reason I have anything right now."

She frowns. "What are you talking about?"

A heavy sigh escapes me. "We went to a huge party at his frat house sophomore year. I drove us there but still had a couple of drinks. Not a ton, but enough that I was probably just barely over the limit and never should've been behind the wheel. But when you're in college, you think you're invincible. That nothing can touch you. On the way home, we were laughing at something—I can't even remember what it was now—and I ran a stop sign. The next thing I knew, cop lights were going off behind me and I freaked. I would've lost my spot on the team if I got a DUI."

Her eyes light with understanding. "And therefore your chance at the NFL."

I nod sadly. "I was driving Drew's SUV—"

"With the illegal tinting…" She nibbles on her lip, her expression telling me she knows where this is going.

"Drew swapped places with me, and by the time the cop got to the car, he was in the driver's seat."

"That was why my dad took his car away." I can tell immediately when all the puzzle pieces from that year come together for her. She was a sophomore in high school, and her dad gave her Drew's car, which was probably the nicest thing he'd ever done for her. But Emma's never been stupid, and she asked Drew about it more than once. We had sworn that we'd never talk about it, and we didn't.

Panic and guilt seize in my chest realizing that Drew kept our secret this whole time, which only adds another layer of hurt to my betrayal. But Emma needs to understand how hard this is for me. I need her to know I'm not trying to hurt her by not telling her brother. It's all just really complicated.

"My coach got wind of it, but because I wasn't driving, I basically got a slap on the hand." I grip her hands tighter, my eyes imploring her to understand. "I'd have nothing if Drew hadn't switched seats. And it was his idea. The thought had never even occurred to me, but even in his drunken state, he put me first. He realized I had more to lose, and he took the hit. And I'm going to repay him by dating his sister who's always been off-limits? It doesn't sit well with me, Em.

"But I can't stop what we're doing. I don't want to. I know you're pissed at me for not being able to tell him yet, but hopefully now you understand why I'm having such a hard time. I'm about to betray him after he's done so much for me. I'm just trying to figure out a way to keep you both, because I can't lose either of you."

Without hesitation, she wraps her arms around my neck and hugs me tight. My arms slide around her waist, holding her to me as close as I can, the warmth of her body a balm to the turmoil in my soul.

It's strange how one person can be both the source of your guilt and your freedom.

"I get it now," she whispers against my ear.

I hold her against me, hoping she can sense how much she means to me—more than I'm even ready to admit out loud.

TWENTY-NINE

Emma

"Hey Squish, what's up? How's LA?"

I fold my legs underneath me on the couch and get comfortable. "It's good."

"How's the music stuff going? Any luck with that producer?"

My body stiffens, my brain fighting against the memories of what happened with Jason in an attempt at self-preservation. I push away the memories, but that only makes room for the guilt I feel at never telling Drew about what happened. This is another lie—a lie of omission, but it's still a lie—and it's making me sick to my stomach keeping so much from my brother when we've always been honest with each other.

"It didn't work out," I say, hoping he'll let it drop but knowing him well enough to know I'm probably not that lucky.

"What does that mean?" His tone is noticeably chillier as his protective big brother instinct comes out.

I scrub my hand over my forehead. "Don't worry about it. It just didn't work out."

"I'm not dumb, Emma. Did that guy try something?"

"Drew—"

"You better not be about to tell me to drop it again, cause that's not happening, so you better start talking."

The idea of unloading one of my secrets and taking some of the weight off my burdened soul would be nice, but I wish it wasn't this specific secret that I was being forced to talk about. My pulse beats a rapid staccato in my veins, and my chest starts to feel heavy and tight as panic sets in. I close my eyes, but all I see is the recording studio, so I snap them back open and remind myself that I'm safe.

I take a deep breath and try to calm my heart. It's been a month, and I have been doing great. I don't understand why it seems to be hitting me all over again now.

I pinch my nose before responding, trying to find a way to frame this in such a way that won't cause my brother to jump on a plane and come straight here.

"He...he got a little aggressive, but I'm fine. I promise. I said no and he backed off." I leave out the part where he shoved his hands between my legs first and I had to say no multiple times.

He's quiet for what feels like a full minute. "Does Luke know?" I can't read his tone, which worries me.

"Yeah, he's the one who picked me up."

"And he let that fucker live?" Okay, I can definitely read his tone now. He's pissed. I try to calm him down the best I can.

"Drew, I begged him to take me home, and he focused on me. Would you rather he focused on some guy who doesn't matter anymore?"

"What do you mean he focused on you? You said this ass-wipe backed off."

Shit.

"Emma, I swear to God..."

"Okay, he got a little handsy before he backed off. I promise I'm fine. Luke came and got me. He was just as pissed as you sound and definitely wanted to rip Jason apart, but I wanted to get out of there, so he took me home. That's it. End of story."

My brother mutters, and I'd swear he said he needed to have a word with Luke. I decide to change the subject, hoping I can keep my brother from planning someone's murder from two states away—or at all.

"Luke's got everything handled. He's been great, actually," I say, my voice soft and tender as I fiddle with the couch cushion and fondly remember the way he bent me over and fucked me silly on this couch just yesterday.

Drew hesitates before responding. "You're not trying to hit on my best friend, are you?" His tone tells me he's horrified by the idea, and my stomach sinks.

"No."

It's not technically a lie. I'm not *trying*.

He lets out a relieved sigh that causes dread to settle heavily in my gut. "Thank God. That would be so fucking awkward. I know you had a crush on him when you were younger, but come on, Em."

My hackles rise. "Come on? What's that supposed to mean?"

"It's never gonna happen. He knows better than to hook up with you. It's bro code. He'd never break my trust that way, so there's no sense in pining for him. Honestly, I thought you were over that stupid crush."

His words hurt me, but I can't let him know that. Clearing my throat, I respond, "Yeah, I am." The words taste like ash in my mouth. I hate lying to my brother, but after his latest remark, I better understand Luke's concerns.

He's right. Drew's not ready for us to tell him the truth. But what worries me most is that I'm not sure he'll ever be ready.

"Close your eyes." Luke's husky voice whispers against my hair while his front presses against my back, and his arms cage me to my dresser where I was searching for a top to wear with my skin-tight high-waisted black capri pants. I instantly follow his instructions, my body already vibrating with excitement at what he might possibly have planned.

"Do you know how sexy you are?" I nod my head and can feel his grin with his cheek pressed against the curve of my neck. His lips press soft kisses along my skin.

"God, you're tempting, but this isn't why I came in here."

"Why did you come in here then?" My voice is breathy, and I couldn't hide my response to him even if I tried.

He steps back, and I immediately miss the warmth of his body. "I have a surprise for you."

I turn around to see a giant grin on his handsome face. He's wearing a pair of well-fitted jeans and a dark blue long-sleeved shirt that hugs the muscles of his biceps and hides the tattoos that I've traced with my tongue. His hazel eyes slide down from my face and immediately turn heated when he sees me from the front standing before him in just my tight black capri pants that accentuate my ass and a black lace bra that does nothing to hide my lush cleavage.

His jaw slides back and forth, and he bites his lip as his gaze comes back to mine. He steps forward, his hand sliding around my neck and tugging me to him. His lips brush mine in a sultry kiss that leaves me panting when he pulls away again.

"I'm having a hard time keeping my hands off of you."

"Then don't."

He smirks at my reply but shakes his head and steps away again. If he thinks the distance will ease the tension between us, he's mistaken. I still feel the pull, like two magnets constantly being drawn to each other.

"So you said you have a surprise for me?"

His face lights up again. "Yeah. Come on. Get dressed and meet me downstairs. Bring your guitar."

My smile falls from my face, but he doesn't see it because he's already turned around and is walking out my bedroom door. I chew on my lip and glance over at my guitar, resting in its case where it's been for the last several days. I haven't been able to even pick it up. For the first time in my life, there are no melodies or words floating through my head. It's like any creative juices I had have completely abandoned me, leaving me feeling empty and lost.

I sigh heavily, then grab a soft, fitted teal sweater from my drawer and finish getting dressed. I meet Luke downstairs as he requested, guitar in hand and my anxiety clawing at my throat.

He looks giddy, like a kid at Christmas, so I quickly paste a smile on my face and hope he doesn't see the cracks in my exterior. He walks up to me and pulls out a black blindfold that looks just like the one he used when he surprised me by taking me to the Hollywood Bowl.

I quirk my brow and shoot him a look. "Taking me to another venue to perform?"

I ignore the quick spike in my heart rate at the thought of having to play when I can hardly stand to hold my guitar.

"Not quite." He looks at me closely, his gaze soft and gentle as his eyes connect with mine. "Do you trust me?"

"Yes." I don't even have to think about it.

He smiles. "Good. Now, close your eyes."

I do as he asks and feel the blindfold over my eyes. He guides me to his car and helps to buckle me in. "We'll be there in about forty minutes if traffic is on our side."

"And where is *there* exactly?"

"Nope. You're not gonna get me to spill that easily."

I slide my right hand along the side of my thigh and squeeze as tight as I can, hoping Luke can't tell what I'm doing. The longer we drive, the more I grip the bottom of my thigh, hoping the pressure will help relieve some of my anxiety. By the time the car stops, I'm a ball of nerves and have to actively remind myself to breathe. I'm so confused about why I'm feeling this way. I've never struggled with anxiety like this before. But I've also never lost my music before either.

Everything feels off.

My door opens and Luke's scent—all man—filters through my nose. Comfort washes over me like ocean water brushing across my feet on the beach. He grabs my hand and guides me inside.

An unfamiliar voice speaks up. "Can I help you, sir?" There's a hesitancy in his tone, and I wonder if it's because Luke is huge and he just walked in with a woman blindfolded.

Probably seems a bit sketch to an unknown observer.

"I'm here to see Trent Bridger. He's expecting us."

Wait. Did he just say Trent Bridger? Lead singer of the rock band Rapturous Intent?

How the hell does Luke know Trent?

"Oh, you're Luke Carter! Yes, right this way."

Luke gently cups his hand around my elbow and guides me through the building. "Um, Luke. Can I take the blindfold off now?"

"Not quite." I can hear the smile in his voice. He's excited about this, and my heart plummets to my stomach because I'm more certain than ever that I'm going to dread what he's got up his sleeve. But I don't want to disappoint Luke. I don't want him to see me as weak. So I throw back my shoulders and dig deep for the strength to get through this and pretend I'm as excited about this surprise as he is.

"Okay. You ready?" Luke moves behind me and places both hands on my shoulders, stopping me in place. He gently removes the blindfold, and it takes a moment for my eyes to adjust before I'm hit in the gut with an unexpected wave of nausea. We're standing in the middle of a recording studio with Trent Bridger standing at the board with another guy I don't recognize but assume is his producer.

Trent turns to us with a warm and welcoming smile on his face, but my feet are frozen in place as my gaze slides around the room. Luke peeks around from behind me to see my reaction, and Trent laughs, completely misinterpreting my shock.

"I get that a lot. You should've seen Gina the first time she met me." I remember meeting a woman named Gina at Jack and Paige's wedding. She's engaged to Will Edmonson, another player on Luke's team.

Luke wraps his arm around my shoulder and pulls me against his side. He looks down at me as he explains. "Trent grew up with Will, and when I was talking in the locker room about your interest in becoming a singer, Will offered to connect me with him." Luke glances up at Trent. "And he was more than happy to help you out and hear what you've got."

Luke leans into me conspiratorially and whispers, "I may have told him you're about to be the next big hit, so no pressure." He laughs, having no idea that the weight of his words is suffocating.

What is wrong with me? I've never dreaded singing like this. I don't understand what's going on.

I wipe my sweaty palms on my jeans and then extend a hand to Trent. He accepts it quickly, his grip firm but not overpowering. "So, what do you say? I've got my favorite producer, Pete, here today to record for us. Wanna get in there and show us what you've got?"

"Uh...sure." What else am I supposed to say? If I say no, Luke will be disappointed in me, and I can't stand the idea of him not looking at me like I'm capable of anything.

Trent turns to Pete, who's fiddling with the controls on the board. Luke's phone rings, and he digs in his pocket and then glances at the screen.

"Shoot. It's my agent, who's been working on nailing down a sponsorship deal. I gotta take this." He glances at Trent and Pete who are turned away from us before dropping a kiss to my forehead. "I'll be right back."

My shoulders sag in relief when he leaves the room. I need a minute without him looking at me so I can try to firm up my resolve and get over whatever the hell is happening in my head. I close my eyes and try some simple breathing techniques that have always helped me when my parents were causing me stress or anxiety, but it still doesn't help.

"Emma?"

I open my eyes to see Trent's expectant expression. "You want to get set up in the room?"

"Sure thing."

I grab my guitar case, which Luke left at the door, with shaky hands and go into the studio. I place my guitar on the floor and bend over to unlatch the case. The minute my fingers touch the neck of my guitar, my body completely freezes as unexplainable fear washes over me, pulling me down until I feel like I'm drowning.

I can't move. I can't breathe.

Water spots fall on my guitar. Where is water coming from? A horrible keening sound fills my ears, but I still can't move, and I can't figure out where the sound is coming from either.

Black spots suddenly fill my vision before the whole world disappears.

THIRTY

Luke

"Luke!"

I spin around, my phone clutched to my ear as my agent talks on the other end about the deal he's just closed. The second I see Trent's panicked expression, I end the call and run to him.

"What's wrong?"

"I don't know. Emma just lost it." He fills me in as we race back into the studio. "She bent over her guitar and then just started crying and screaming before she passed out."

My concerned gaze lands on Emma's limp body on the floor. Her face is ashen and her eyes closed, but the streaks from her tears are noticeable. I rush to her side and drop to my knees, pulling her into my arms while my hands caress her face.

"Emma. Fuck. Em, wake up." I brush wet strands of hair from her face and realize that her forehead is covered in cold sweat.

She seemed fine when I left to take my phone call. I spin my head around and glare at Trent. "What the fuck happened?"

He shakes his head, shock covering his face. "I have no idea. She seemed fine in the booth and even when she walked in here. It wasn't until she opened her guitar case that she lost it. I have no clue what happened. It's like she was triggered by something, but I can't figure out what."

His words penetrate through my fear for Emma's well-being, and all the blood drains from my face. Triggered.

I look around the room we're in and wonder if it reminded her of Jason's studio.

Fuck.

Fuck, fuck, fuck. I messed this up. Was she panicked before we even got here? Why didn't she say anything?

Trent must see the remorse and regret on my face. "Do you know what happened?"

I nod my head and close my eyes. I can't believe I was so stupid. "I'm pretty sure, yeah."

"Feel like filling me in? Cause I've never seen anything like this."

How much do I tell him? It's Emma's story to share. Would she want another person to know she was assaulted? Does he even know who Jason is?

"Do you know Jason Berker?"

Trent's gaze turns murderous. "She worked with that fucker?"

I nod.

He slides his fingers through his hair and lets out a soft groan. "Fucking A, I hate that guy, but no one will do what it takes to end his career, even knowing what they do about his behavior. He's a predator of the worst kind. Fuck, Luke, I'm sorry. I never would've just thrown her into this if I had known she'd worked with him. I would've made sure she was comfortable."

I shake my head, trying to ease his worries. "You didn't know." Hell, I knew about the situation, and I still didn't realize how badly this would affect her.

Pete comes in with a bottle of water. "The paramedics are on their way to check her over and make sure she's okay, but if she can drink some water that might help. I also have a chocolate bar in my bag if you want it."

I take the bottle and set it beside me. She's still passed out, so there's no sense in trying to get her to drink right now. I brush my fingers across her cheek, which is thankfully starting to pink up again. My gaze follows my fingers before I hear a throat clear behind me, and I glance back to see Trent watching us carefully.

"How long have you two been together?"

"It's..." I know I should deny it, but I can't. Not while I have her in my arms. "Things are a bit complicated."

"You said she's your best friend's sister."

"She is."

I expect judgment, but instead all I see is understanding in his gaze. There's a story there, but I don't ask because now's not the time.

Right now, the only thing that matters is Emma.

She has to be okay, or I'll never forgive myself.

"You know, I worked with a singer who also...struggled after working with Jason."

He says struggled like that's the polite way of saying she had PTSD.

He continues, "She told me a little bit of what happened with him, and then all the ways she lost control after because she felt like what happened to her was her fault. She started using drugs, sex, alcohol—anything to dull the trauma of what she went through. It wasn't until she almost died from an overdose before she finally admitted she needed help. She started seeing a therapist who really helped her turn things around." He hesitates before adding, "I could reach out to her and get the number of the therapist for Emma."

"I don't know if that's necessary." My family, and Emma's,

have always seen therapy as something only weak people needed. It wasn't until I saw what it did for Will that I realized how backwards that thinking was.

The strongest people in the world are the ones who know when to ask for help.

One glance down at Emma, and I know I'll do anything to help her get through this. I've never been so scared as I was when I saw her lying on the floor looking one minute away from death.

I look back up at Trent. "Actually, uh, yeah. I think Emma would appreciate that."

He nods his head and then digs in his pants pocket for his phone. "I'll give Sadie a call now."

He exits the room right as Emma starts to stir in my arms. "Luke?" Her voice is soft and hoarse, her eyes bleary.

I hug her to my chest, fighting the unfamiliar emotions that are nearly overwhelming me. "Fuck, Em, you scared the shit out of me."

Her arms wrap around me, and she squeezes me tight. "I'm so sorry."

I pull back slightly so I can look at her. "What the hell are you sorry for? I'm the one that didn't think this through. I should've thought about how you would feel being back in a recording studio."

She frowns at me. "You think this has to do with Jason?"

"Doesn't it?"

She stares at my chest, her eyes unfocused as I watch her thinking it through, then she sags against me, and tears flood her eyes. "I can't believe I never realized that."

Now I'm confused. "What do you mean?"

She looks at me, guilt in her eyes. "I haven't been able to pick up my guitar for days. I used to hear music in my head all the time, whether it was words or a melody, but lately, there's been nothing. Not a thing. I couldn't figure out what was wrong, and I never once realized it could be about Jason. I mean, that happened over a month ago. I just thought something was wrong with me."

I move my hands from around her waist to grip her face. "There is absolutely nothing wrong with you. Do you understand me? You are perfect just as you are, and none of this is your fault."

Tears fill her vision as she collapses against me, her sobs slowly breaking my heart as her tears soak through my shirt.

Emma's head rests on my chest as we cuddle in my bed. The drive home was a blur, and the second we got in the house, I grabbed her hand and brought her straight to my room. We've been lying here, cuddled together ever since.

Her hand slides from where it's resting on my stomach, across my chest, and reaches up, grasping me behind my neck. My eyes meet hers as she pulls my mouth down to kiss her, and I give in to her silent plea. The kiss starts out soft before turning needy and consuming.

I'm out of breath when she breaks away and stares into my eyes.

"Make me forget," she whispers.

"What?"

She closes her eyes as if in pain. "Ever since you mentioned it might be because of Jason, I've been thinking about that day. I keep remembering his hands on my body, and I don't want to think of him. I only want memories of how you touch me." Her hand grips my neck again as she pleads, "Touch me. Please."

I can't deny her anything, but I also think she needs to be in control right now. Gripping her hips, I slide her body until she's lying on top of me, her legs automatically hugging my hips. She can no doubt feel what her kiss did to me.

My gaze caresses her face as my fingers slide through her soft red locks. She sits up, her hands resting on my chest while she starts grinding against me. I fight back a groan, but fuck, it feels amazing.

"Luke." Her voice is breathless and soft, but it hits me right in the heart to hear the need behind it. "Touch me."

"I am touching you."

"More. I need more," she says as she pulls off her sweater and her bra in the blink of an eye.

It's like she sets off a beast inside me with those words. Suddenly, my hands are everywhere. They slide down her neck, relishing her porcelain smooth skin and tracing across her gorgeous freckles. When I reach her taut, rosy-pink nipples, I can't stop myself from pinching them, which elicits the sexiest sound from her throat. She throws her head back, her hips rocking back and forth faster against me when I cover her nipples with my mouth and suck hard. My hands caress every inch of her body while my mouth ravishes her breasts like they're the best thing I've ever had in my mouth.

"Take off your pants," she says as she slides off me and wiggles out of her pants and underwear. Once I strip off my shirt and kick off my pants and boxers, she gets back into posi-tion on top of me.

Her warm, slick pussy grinds against my rock-hard dick, and I drop my head back, groaning. Our heavy breathing fills the room. When she grips my cock and positions it right at her entrance, all I can do is stare at her, my body already primed to detonate. The second my tip starts to enter her, she drops her body down, her pussy sucking my dick inside her like that's where it's always belonged.

Fuck me, nothing has ever felt so good.

I grip Emma's neck, pulling her attention from where we're joined to meet my gaze. With our eyes locked, I pump into her, meeting her thrusts with my own and losing myself in her green eyes.

"Don't ever stop," she says breathlessly.

I shake my head, unable to speak, my body fighting back my release until I make her come. Her eyes fill with tears the longer they remain locked on mine, and my chest aches at the pain there. Then the tears release and cascade down her cheeks, making me want to do whatever it takes to ensure she never feels pain again.

"Please don't let me go." Her voice cracks on the last word and my defenses against her completely crumble. I pull her mouth to mine in a bruising kiss, hoping it tells her all the things I can't say with words.

I'm hers.

She owns me completely.

I love you.

I feel my orgasm coming on fast, and her pelvis grinds harder against me, chasing her own orgasm. Her body quivers and shakes on top of me as her orgasm hits her, the convulsions of her pussy quickly pulling my orgasm out of me. She drops on top of me, her legs still slightly shaking against my hips from the aftershocks. I wrap my arms around her and kiss the top of her head.

Her breathing evens out quickly, and I know she's asleep without having to look. But I'm wide awake, realization crashing into me now that I'm not lost in the euphoria of being intimately connected with Emma.

I love her.

I'm in love with her. No falling about it. I've fallen. I'm done. I'm hers.

I doubt any of that will make a difference to Drew. He's just going to see my betrayal, and I can't even blame him. I've broken all the rules of bro code here. Not only have I gotten together with his sister, but I lied about it. My gut twists painfully as I acknowledge that I've turned into what I always swore I wouldn't—a liar.

I hold Emma closer to me, her broken voice pleading for me not to let her go echoing in my head. I don't want to let her go. I can't let her go. I can only hope that when I finally get the courage to tell Drew that he understands.

THIRTY-ONE

Emma

"How do you feel about that?" Jane asks.

My fingers fidget with the fringe on the throw pillow at my new therapist's office. Thankfully, Jane was able to fit me in right away. I've been seeing her twice a week for three weeks, and even though this is only my sixth session with her, we've covered a lot. She makes it really easy to be open with her.

That, or I just couldn't keep everything inside me anymore.

Our first two sessions, I spewed out the whole story of my assault like it was being purged from my system. We also talked about how I'd been censoring myself when talking about my assault with Luke and Drew. I was trying to make them more comfortable, but the reality is it's an uncomfortable topic. After that, we delved into what happened at the recording studio with Trent and what she refers to as my delayed trauma response over what happened with Jason. I'd never thought about it in those terms. I always assumed if I was going to have an extreme reaction, it would've happened immediately. Apparently, it's not all that uncommon for someone to experience their trauma weeks—and sometimes even months—after it's happened.

Today, we started by talking about my struggle to play

guitar, something that I still can't seem to do. But then I made mention of the stress with Luke and my brother, and that took our conversation in a completely different direction.

"Emma? How do you feel about the fact that Luke still hasn't told Drew about you two?"

I pull my gaze from the window and back to her. "I hate it," I say softly. "I've never lied to my brother. He's always been my biggest supporter, even when my parents tried to pit us against each other with all that *why can't you be more like your brother* bullshit. He never pushed me to be anything but who I was. He encouraged my love of music, even if he didn't quite understand my passion. He snuck me out of the house so I could go to music lessons which he helped pay for by chipping in his allowance.

"Drew's always had my back, and keeping this from him is killing me." A tear slowly escapes my eye, but I hold the rest back, not wanting to completely lose it in Jane's office—again. I know I'm a crier and an overly emotional person, but even I'm getting sick of the tears.

"Have you shared these feelings with Luke?"

I shake my head. "No. I know where he stands. He's not ready to tell Drew, or at least he doesn't know *how* to tell him."

She tilts her head ever so slightly. "Why haven't you told Drew?"

I look at her, confused. "I told you, Luke wants to be the one to tell him."

"Do you think Drew would want to hear this from his best friend or from his sister, who he's always looked out for?" she asks softly. I ponder her question for a moment, not sure how to answer. "Do you think it's possible he might respond more posi-tively if it comes from you?" she asks.

"Honestly, I haven't even really considered that. Not after Luke shared everything that went down between them in college. It just seemed so important to him that he was the one to tell Drew."

"But based on our conversations, that's made you feel like a secret, or something he's possibly ashamed of."

"It has," I say, my voice small, because telling her was the first time I'd said it out loud, and the truth of the words made me feel both free and trapped at the same time. Free because I was finally being honest but trapped because I didn't see anything I could really do about it.

"But Luke will probably be mad at me if I go around him."

"That's possible, and perhaps even likely," she says, cocking her head thoughtfully to the side. "But how do you think you'll feel if you tell Drew?"

I don't even have to think about it. "Better. I'd feel better. I can't stand lying to my brother anymore. I've had a knot in my stomach for weeks every time he's called me, and I can't stand it."

She gives me a sympathetic smile. "Then I think that's your answer."

"You think I should tell Drew."

"I think honesty is important to you, and this is an aspect of your life you have control over. After everything you've been through in the past couple of months, I think you deserve to prioritize yourself and your needs."

Telling Drew would take a lot of stress off my plate. Deceiving him is eating away at me, and a lie of omission is still a lie.

Nerves flit around my stomach as the phone rings and I wait for him to pick up. My palms are a sweaty mess, and my heart rate is through the roof, but I have to do this for my sanity.

"Hey, Squish. How's life in sunny SoCal?"

"Warm."

He laughs, and the warmth of his voice brings a soft smile to my face. "Anything's warm after you've lived in Seattle."

"Very true."

Silence fills the line. I don't know how to say this.

"So, what's up?" Drew asks.

"I need to tell you something."

"Okay," he says, dragging out the word.

"But you have to promise not to get mad."

Silence. Then he says, "Okay, you've got my attention now, Em. What's going on?"

"Do you promise not to get mad?"

"I promise to try."

I nibble my lip thinking that's probably going to be the best I'll get out of him. "Fine. Um...are you sitting down?"

"Just spit it out, Emma," he says curtly, on edge.

"I'm dating Luke."

Nothing. The silence drags on so long I check my phone to make sure he's still on the line. He is.

"Drew?" I ask cautiously, my nerves now a riot in my gut. "Say something."

"How..." His voice breaks and I know my brother well enough that I can practically see him trying to keep his cool. "How long?"

I close my eyes in defeat, knowing this is the part that will hurt him the most. "A little over a month."

I hear a loud bang on the other end and jump. "Drew?"

"He's my best friend, Emma! He had one goddamn job and that was to look out for you, not to *fuck* you." He spits out the words like he's disgusted and livid.

"It's not like that. This isn't a meaningless fling or just a hookup thing." I take a breath, searching for my courage and trying to remind myself that this is my brother, and he's always loved me and supported me.

"I love him."

"That's not news, Emma. You've always been in love with him, but do you honestly think he loves you?" His tone is scathing, but his voice catches on the last word, almost like the idea is unbearable.

My breath halts in my chest as insecurity infiltrates my body. Luke hasn't said the words, and suddenly I'm second-guessing my decision to tell Drew. Tears instantly flood my eyes and cascade down my pale cheeks, and I don't even bother to be embarrassed about how quickly he's made me cry.

I try to find my voice. "We didn't want to hurt you—"

"Well, you fucking did. And if you think you mean anything to him, you're kidding yourself. If you meant something to him, he would've told me. He would've been honest with me, Emma. Luke's never lied to me before—*never*—so if he lied about this then that in itself tells me how little you really mean to him." He huffs out a humorless laugh. "And clearly how little I mean to him. Fuck! I can't talk about this anymore."

Silence fills the line, and this time when I pull the phone away, I can see that Drew hung up on me.

But his words linger, surrounding me until I hear them on an endless loop in my head. They magnify all my greatest insecurities, leaving me feeling like a greater mess than I was before. A small voice tries to break through and say that my brother was hurting and lashing out, but his words were too close to all the doubts I already heard in my head about why Luke hadn't told Drew. No one knows Luke better than Drew, so he has to be right about this, right?

Oh my God. What the fuck have I done?

THIRTY-TWO

Luke

The locker room is full of grumbling after our loss against the Seahawks. A few complaints about the bad referees make the rounds, but the reality is we played like shit today. They won fair and square.

We didn't deserve a victory after all our fuckups.

I pass Gabe Romero on the way to my cubby which is just a few down from his. Normally, I'd give him a pat on the back, but I'm fucking pissed over our loss. I can see he's beating himself up over the loss too. He got injured last game and was out on injured reserve, so he's taking the loss personally. To be fair, losing a member of the Fierce Four definitely didn't help things, but Jack also couldn't catch a break tonight, and the Seahawks defense shut us down in damn near every play.

Even if Gabe had been able to play, I doubt the outcome would be any different.

He turns to me. "Are you bringing Emma to the team party happening next weekend? It's going to be at that new club that just opened. Apparently, it's going to be the biggest event of the season."

Yeah, and crawling with paparazzi because of all the other

celebrities that got invited to that party. It's not just a team party with only Wolves players and their partners. It's an excuse to rub elbows with the rich and famous. So as much as I wish I could walk in there with Emma on my arm, I know it's a disaster waiting to happen. The odds of our picture being taken and Drew seeing it are too high to risk.

"Probably not."

He frowns. "Why the hell not?"

"Emma and I are keeping things quiet right now." Fuck, I really don't want to talk about this. I'm already in a piss-poor mood. I just want to change and go home where I can stew over our loss and my own fuckups in peace.

"But you brought her to Jack's wedding."

"Yeah, but there wasn't a flock of vultures there hunting down a scandalous picture. Emma and I..." I grip the back of my neck. "Her brother is my best friend, and he wouldn't be okay with us being together."

He arches his eyebrow and looks at me curiously. "You mean to tell me you've been seeing that woman in hiding?"

"Yep, pretty much."

He shakes his head, his disappointment obvious. "Listen, I know I barely know Emma, but even I can tell that's not the kind of woman you keep hidden. That's the kind of woman you show off with pride because you can't believe you're the lucky bastard who gets to stand beside her." He shakes his head again. "For what it's worth, I think you're making a mistake, and I really hope for your sake you figure it out before you lose her for good. That's not a woman who settles for a man who hides her like a dirty little secret."

Nausea hits me like a punch to the gut, his words finding their mark and making me feel like the lowest scum.

He's right.

Emma's not that kind of woman. She deserves so much

more, but I still haven't figured out how to best tell Drew. I try to push aside the doubt that now feels like it's permeating every pore in my body telling me my time to figure it out is almost up.

⬤

Drew's name pops up on the display in my car right as I pull into my garage. Fuck, I am really not in the mood for this. It's been a super shitty night, and I'm already in a bad mood, but seeing Drew's name just reminds me of the secret that's slowly suffocating me.

Gabe's right. I need to tell Drew. I can't keep hiding Emma. Maybe him calling me is fate's way of giving me the chance to finally tell him the truth.

Fuck, he's going to hate me, and I wish he wasn't calling me when I'm already in a shit headspace, but I need to do this.

I hit accept. "Hey, man, I'm glad you called. I—" I don't even get the chance to tell him I need to talk to him about some-thing before his rage-filled voice cuts me off.

"You fucking asshole! I can't believe you'd do this to me. *Me* of all people. After all the shit we've been through."

My stomach drops. He knows. How the hell does he know?

"You piece of shit. I asked you to take care of her, not sleep with her. I *told you* no!"

Shit. "Drew—"

"No. You're going to listen to me. Emma told me every-thing." Wait, *Emma* told him? What the fuck? She knew this was important to me.

What the fuck did she say?

Anger starts to bubble beneath my surface—both at Emma for telling Drew without talking to me about it first or even giving me a fucking heads-up, and at Drew for not letting me explain my side of things.

"My sister is off-limits. I made that perfectly clear from the very beginning. I can't believe you did this. I can't believe you're willing to throw away our friendship just so you can get your fucking rocks off. She's my *fucking sister*, Luke! You could've had anyone else. I can't believe you. I just...fuck you, man. Fuck you for shitting all over our friendship. It's great to see what I really mean to you."

He hangs up before I even have a chance to respond, and my anger flares even more. I stomp into the house, throwing my bag on the floor and making my way into the living room in search of Emma. I find her on the couch on the phone, her eyes red and swollen, her cheeks blotchy.

"Bernie, I gotta call you back." She drops the phone and stands up. "Luke, I have to tell you something."

I wave my cell phone in the air. "That you told your brother about us, even after I explained to you why I wanted to fucking do it." There's no way she missed the venom in my voice if her small flinch is any indication.

"I've just lost my best friend, Emma. Is that what you wanted? What the fuck were you thinking? You couldn't even give me a heads-up before you messed everything up? What the fuck!" I grip my hands in my hair, my anger at this whole situation boiling over. I can't even look at her right now. I don't know why I even came in the house. I should've just left. Gone to the team gym to blow off some steam. Called Matt. Something. Anything but standing here with her when she just fucked us both.

"Why would you do it?" I ask, because I told her over and over how important it was to me that I be the one to tell him.

Her mouth opens to respond, but I cut her off, shaking my head. "You know what? It doesn't matter. You just screwed us both. I hope you're happy. FUCK! I can't believe you did this. How stupid can you be, Emma?"

I know the instant the words leave my mouth that I've gone too far, but I can barely see past my anger at this point.

She closes her eyes briefly before opening them and staring me down. The spark that always lights up her green eyes is gone, and in its place is cold anger.

"Fuck. You." She spits each word. "Lying to him was killing me, but you didn't give a shit about that, did you? All you cared about was your friendship with him. Well, what about my relationship with him? Do you know I've never once lied to Drew? But I did for you. And you have the nerve to come in here and call me stupid and blame me because you didn't have the balls to tell him. It's been over a month, Luke! What the fuck were you waiting for?"

She laughs, but it's hollow, and her eyes are sad, her voice no longer filled with fury but resignation. "Drew was right. I never meant anything to you."

She looks away from me, shaking her head before she turns back to me. "You were never going to tell him about us, were you? It was never real. I was just convenient." Her shoulders sag, and her heartbreak is clear as day on her face, along with acceptance. "You're right, Luke. I was stupid."

She walks out of the room, making sure to keep her distance so our bodies don't touch when she walks past me. I'm frozen in place, her words trying to penetrate my haze of anger, but struggling.

Everything's falling apart, and I don't know how to deal with all these feelings. I can't stay here. I need to release some of this rage so I don't say or do anything else I'll regret.

I thrust my arms up, the weight more than I'm used to, but the burn is the only thing that's finally taking away some of the anger that's consumed me. It's not usually advised to work out after a game, but fuck it.

The more I push my body, the more the anger turns into the emotion that was driving it all along—heartbreak.

I just lost my best friend, the guy that's always had my back, my brother, my lifeline. But worst of all, I think I just lost the woman I'm in love with too.

My words to her cycle through my mind on repeat, and I feel nothing but shame at how I spoke to her. No matter how angry I was with the situation, Emma didn't deserve that.

I hear her words in my head, and now that I'm not seeing red, the memory of her face when she said them penetrates my soul, leaving me feeling more broken than I ever have before.

How did I fuck this up so badly?

I set the weight back on the rack and sit up, my elbows resting on my knees and my head in my hands. What am I going to do to fix this?

"You okay?"

My heart rate spikes as I look up to see Will. "Fuck, dude, you scared the shit out of me. I didn't hear you come in."

He frowns down at me. "Sorry. I thought you heard me when the door slammed shut. You okay? You look like shit."

"Gee, thanks."

"You still didn't answer my question."

"No, I'm not okay." I drop my head into my hands again. "I fucked everything up."

"With Emma?" he asks sympathetically.

I nod. "And with Drew."

"What happened?"

Where do I even begin? I decide to tell him the whole sordid story so he understands the level of how badly I've messed this all up. He sits against the wall across from me while I talk. He doesn't interrupt except to ask clarifying questions, but even then, he keeps them short and to the point. There's no judgment. He just listens. When I'm done, he lets out a heavy sigh.

"Damn, that's a mess," he says.

I nod in agreement.

"Well, I know a little something about fucking up with a woman and saying shit I didn't mean." He looks at me knowingly and reminds me of how he messed up with Gina.

"How'd you fix it? I feel like I can't go home until I know how to approach Emma."

"Honestly? I fought like hell for her. I got my head straight and worked through my shit. It didn't happen overnight, and I'm lucky she even gave me a second look after I messed up with her, but I make sure she never questions how much I love her. I don't just tell her every day, I show her."

"Emma doesn't know."

"That you love her?"

I nod. "I've never said it, let alone felt it for a woman. My parents' marriage was a disaster. I wasn't sure I'd ever actually fall in love after watching them constantly tear each other apart. I didn't even think love truly existed." A small smile tugs at the corner of my mouth. "But I never stood a chance with Emma. It's impossible not to love her."

I never meant anything to you.

It was never real.

I was just convenient.

Her words stab at my heart. She thinks she didn't mean anything to me when the reality is she means more to me than anyone else in my life.

Even more than Drew.

She's everything.

I feel sick to my stomach knowing she thinks she's anything less than my whole fucking world.

I have to tell her I love her.

I have to fight for her and show her.

Maybe someday Drew will forgive me, but all that matters now is Emma's forgiveness.

I can't live without her.

THIRTY-THREE

Emma

The door slams, and I hear Luke's car pull out of the garage. I desperately wish I could stop the tears, but it feels like my heart's been ripped out and nothing will ease the pain.

I'm so fucking stupid.

Of course Drew was right. He knows Luke. And Luke didn't dispute a single word I said downstairs.

Reality crashes down on me, and I start sobbing so hard I can barely breathe. My legs give out underneath me, the emotional weight of everything literally bringing me to my knees. God, this hurts so much worse than anything else I've ever experienced. I don't know how long I sit there crying, but everything hurts when the tears finally subside, and the house is still quiet, so I know Luke hasn't come back home yet.

What am I going to do when he comes back? I can't stay in this house with him. I can hardly stomach the idea of looking at him after what just happened.

Maybe I can stay with Bernie and double down on finding a new apartment within the week. I'd stopped looking when Luke and I got together, but clearly that was a mistake. All I know is I have to leave before Luke gets back.

I pick up my phone to text her, but it vibrates in my hand with a call from my mom instead.

Seriously? What did I do to piss off the universe so badly? Can't a girl catch a break? I'm not emotionally strong enough to handle a lecture from her telling me how much I don't live up to their standards.

I get it. I'm not enough. That's been made painfully clear tonight. I don't need another reminder.

I hit decline and shoot a text to Bernie, knowing if I call her, she probably won't answer because she hates talking on the phone. She texts me back almost immediately.

Bernie: Of course, hun. You're always welcome. Luke's a dumbass. I'll cue up a Harry Potter marathon just for you.

Remarkably, her words bring a smile to my face. But then my mom's name flashes across the screen again, immediately wiping any traces of my smile. I haven't talked to my mom since I left Seattle. Why does she have to call me tonight of all nights?

I ignore the call again and throw my phone on my bed. I grab a couple of suitcases from my closet and frantically start packing. I have no plans to come back here, so I need to pack as much as I can. I'll have Luke send the rest of my stuff when I get a place so we don't have to actually talk to each other again.

My phone buzzes repeatedly on my bed as I pack until I can't take the incessant interruption. Why can't my mom just let me be miserable in peace? It's like she's got some fucked up radar for when life is beating me down and she needs to add in her two cents.

"What?" I yell into the phone, my patience completely tapped.

"Emma—" My mom's sob instantly changes my mood.

"Mom? What's going on?"

"It's D-Drew," she cries into the phone. "He was in an accident."

All the blood drains from my face as my butt falls to the bed. "What?"

"He was driving home from the gym and someone T-T-boned h-him," she stutters before sobbing uncontrollably.

No.

I've already lost Luke. I can't lose my brother.

"Is he okay?" Fear grips my heart, waiting for her response.

She sobs again, and I hear muffled noise before my dad gets on the line, his voice more tired and defeated than I've ever heard it. "Emma?"

"Dad, is Drew okay?"

"We don't know yet. It...it wasn't good, Emma. There's a lot of damage. He's in surgery now, but they won't tell us much."

My teary gaze lands on the suitcases already packed on my bed, and it becomes clear to me what I should do. I've already lost my music, and now I've lost the only man I've ever been in love with. There's really nothing keeping me in LA anymore.

"I'm coming home. I'll get the first flight to Seattle and call you with the details."

I disconnect the call and immediately text Bernie.

Me: Hey, there's been a change of plans. I need to go to the airport.

Beep.

Beep.

Beep.

"Emma." My mom's whispered voice jars me awake.

"Ow." I wake with a jolt and immediately rub the kink in my neck, the result of sleeping in a chair with my head bent at an uncomfortable angle. My concerned gaze immediately looks around my mom to Drew's hospital bed, relief coming quick when I see he's still breathing.

He's alive.

He got out of surgery right after I got to the hospital. I managed to catch the last flight of the night to Seattle out of LAX. My parents had a car waiting for me, and since it was the middle of the night, it was a quick drive to the hospital.

Drew has four broken ribs, one of which punctured his lung, a broken arm, and a concussion from whiplash. He also suffered some spinal damage that they need to assess once he wakes up to determine if he's paralyzed or will just need extensive physical therapy. They not only had to repair his lung, but also surgically repair his ribs due to the level of damage.

The doctor said he's lucky to be alive, especially given the fact that the driver's side was hit. My parents tried to convince me to go home and rest, but I refused to leave his side. The last time I spoke to Drew he was angry with me. He said hurtful things, yes, but I know my confession also hurt him. The idea that I almost lost my chance to make it right makes me sick to my stomach. I won't leave my brother. Not unless he kicks me out when he wakes up.

And probably not even then.

Security will have to drag me out of here kicking and screaming. Drew needs me, and I won't leave him.

"Here, I brought you some breakfast," Mom says, handing me a breakfast burrito.

"Thanks."

She looks at me thoughtfully before placing a tender kiss on the top of my head. The gesture takes me by surprise. I can't remember the last time my mom did anything tender where I was concerned. Normally, she just criticizes all my choices—my clothes, my weight, my choice in career. I'm amazed she brought me a breakfast burrito instead of a banana since she's always thought I should take dieting more seriously.

I don't know who this woman is, and she's starting to freak me out. She hasn't said one cutting remark since I got here last night.

My gaze lands back on Drew's prone body in the hospital bed. I guess nearly losing one of her children put things in perspective for her.

I know nearly losing Drew did for me at least.

The events of yesterday feel like they happened so long ago or to someone else. I still feel the sting of heartache when I let Luke infiltrate my thoughts, but I try to shut those down as quickly as possible.

"Any change?" I ask her before taking a small bite of my burrito. My appetite has been non-existent since I got the call about Drew's accident, but I know I need to eat.

She shakes her head, her eyes never leaving Drew's body. "The doctor said it could be a while. It's up to Drew now. But he said everything looks good so far, all things considered, so we shouldn't worry yet." She scoffs, "Easier said than done." Her voice cracks, and tears well in her eyes before spilling down her cheeks.

For the first time, I notice she's not wearing any makeup, her normally impeccable complexion blotchy and red. She's wearing a loose gray sweater and jeans—designer, but still different than her outfits of pantsuits or her scrubs and white lab coat. I didn't even know she owned a pair of jeans.

"It's different being on this side of things." Her voice is quiet, reflective. I'm not sure what to say, so I don't say anything, afraid any words from me might cause criticism that I'm not in the mood for.

"You take it for granted—that your child is safe and healthy. It's so easy to live in that bubble where you feel like nothing bad could ever happen to you. As doctors, we were trained on how to approach families when their loved ones are hurt or worse. It's so easy to be detached when it's not your family member. I never…" She shakes her head, her eyes continuing to spill tears that cause my own eyes to water in sympathy. "I never realized how hard it was for the family. How helpless you feel when you can't do anything to save your own child. You never think it could happen to you, but then it does, and suddenly nothing makes sense in the world, but at the same time things seem clearer than ever."

She brushes aside a few of her tears, but it's a useless gesture as more stream down her face. She finally turns to me. "I'm so sorry, Emma. We've always been so hard on you, and really we should've just been grateful you're happy and healthy."

My own tears fall harder in a silent torrent down my face, my breath frozen in my lungs, all my childhood pain just below the surface.

"I'm so, so sorry, honey. I love you so much. You know that, right?" Her eyes plead with me.

"I'm never going to be the perfect child you wanted. I'm never going to be a size two or dedicated to a job that you approve of like Drew." I can't tell her that my music has shriveled up inside me and I don't know if I'll ever get it back. I can't tell her I'm lost and heartbroken and may end up working in corporate America after all because I don't know what else to do.

So instead of giving her hope that I'll suddenly turn into the daughter she's always wanted, I try to see if she really loves me as the daughter I am.

"I know, Emma. And while your father and I wish you were pursuing a career that would be more stable and financially sound, I can understand your passion for music. Drew explained it to us." She rolls her eyes at herself. "God, he explained it so many times I've lost count." She looks back over at his still body, then back at me. I swear this is the first time my mom has seen me. Like really *seen* me. "I get it now," she says softly, but with a hint of urgency, like she hopes it's not too late to salvage our relationship.

Maybe it's not. Only time will tell.

I nod, afraid to say anything that might ruin this moment. My mom reaches out and grabs my hand, clasping it tightly in hers.

A groan from the bed instantly pulls both of our attention. Without thinking about it, I jump up from my chair and rush to Drew's bedside, gripping his hand gently in mine, careful of the scrapes and bruises that are already discoloring his face and arms.

"Drew? Drew, can you hear me?"

He turns his head toward my voice, letting out another groan and opening his eyes, squinting against the dim overhead light. "Emma," he says hoarsely.

"I'll go get his doctor," my mom says as she rushes out the door.

"Drew," I whisper, my voice tight with barely restrained emotion—okay, let's be real, all of the emotion. Tears blur my vision as I grip his hand a little tighter. "I thought I lost you."

In more ways than one.

"What happened?" His scratchy voice makes my heart ache.

"Here, let me get you some water." I turn to the tray where we've kept a pitcher of water, mostly for ourselves while we waited for Drew to wake up, and pour him a glass. Using a spare straw that a nurse left with the pitcher, I place it in front of his mouth and help him grasp the straw with his lips and take a sip.

When he's had enough, he drops his head back to the pillow, his eyes wincing in pain at even that tiny movement. "What happened?" he asks again, his voice less scratchy than before.

"You were in a car accident. Someone T-boned you."

"Everything hurts."

I reach for his hand again, needing the warmth to reassure me I'm not dreaming. My brother's okay. "You almost died," I say, my voice whisper soft.

He doesn't speak, and by the time the doctor comes in, he's fast asleep again.

An hour later, he wakes again, much more alert but still in pain. The doctor examines him thoroughly and reassures my parents and me that he doesn't appear to have any sustaining damage. He'll need physical therapy, but he's not paralyzed. He got lucky.

"Ideally, he should have someone staying with him since he's going to need some assistance for the next few weeks. Does he have anyone?"

My mom and dad both look to each other before my mom replies, "He can move back in with us while he's recovering."

Drew groans and stares unseeingly at the ceiling. Yeah, I bet that idea sounds about as appealing as a root canal.

"I can stay with him."

Drew's head immediately shifts, his eyes staring at me, searching.

"What about LA, honey?" my mom asks.

"I'm moving back to Seattle."

Drew frowns at me but doesn't say anything. My mom turns to him. "Drew, would that work for you?"

I'm on pins and needles waiting for his response. I get the

sense my parents don't know anything about my argument with Drew right before his accident or the fact I've been dating his best friend behind his back for the last month. If he says no and shuts me down, not only will I have to go back to living with my parents, but I'll also have to explain why my brother, who's always been my biggest defender, doesn't want me anywhere near him.

"Yeah, that works for me."

My eyes widen, and my mouth parts in surprise. I honest to God expected him to shut that idea down.

Drew and I stare silently at each other, our eyes both questioning, while my mom turns to the doctor. "Great. When can he be discharged?"

My parents both converse with the doctor, who's also a friend of theirs, getting all the details about Drew's recovery plan. I break the silent stare-off and listen to the recovery instructions since I'll be the one taking care of him.

After the doctor leaves, my mom walks over to Drew and bends down, placing a tender kiss on his head. "We're going to go pick up some dinner for you that tastes better than this hospital food."

Drew offers her a relieved smile. "Thanks, Mom."

My mom starts walking to the door where my dad is waiting for her, but then turns back when she realizes I haven't moved. "Emma, are you coming with us?"

"Actually, Mom, I was hoping Emma could stay and keep me company."

She gives him a soft smile. "Of course, honey. We'll get you both some food and be back soon."

As soon as the door closes, my gaze slides to Drew, his green stare already locked on my face, a slight furrow to his brow.

"You're moving back?"

I shrug and break our eye contact, hoping I can hide the true depth of my heartbreak for a little longer. "There's nothing for me in California."

The silence settles heavily in the room. I finally cave and glance up at Drew to see him watching me with such concern and sadness that my invisible heartbreak tugs at my chest. My eyes sting with tears I fight back like my life depends on it.

His jaw moves side to side before he asks softly, "What about Luke?"

Hearing his name feels like a stampede of elephants is running rampant on my insides, that pesky organ, my heart, its primary target.

I take a deep breath, trying to fortify myself so I can actually speak, but emotion clogs my throat, and no words will come.

Why does getting your heart broken feel so physically painful? Why does it gut you and make you feel like you just got hit by a ten-ton truck that came back for another pass—or forty?

But I guess when you give someone your whole heart, it makes sense that the rest of your body will feel the pain of that loss. It's a vital organ that's essentially been ripped out, or that feels like it has at least.

I wonder if you can ever fully recover from that kind of pain. Or will you always be just a little less than you were before?

Forever doomed to be a little bit broken and missing a piece of yourself.

"Emma?"

"I can't." I choke out the words, my pleading gaze snapping up to his, the tears I've worked so hard to fight back streaming down my face.

Drew doesn't ask about Luke again. Instead, he watches me the rest of the night, through dinner with our parents, and the rest of visiting hours before they finally kick us out. Now that he's awake, they won't let me stay by his side.

I ride in the back of my parents' car, watching the typical Seattle rain come down in torrents and the streetlights flash as we drive past, all the while the concern in Drew's eyes haunting me. Sooner or later, he's going to ask me again about Luke. I know my brother. He's not just going to forget about everything that happened before his accident.

Sooner or later, I'm going to have to admit that I gave myself wholeheartedly to a man who was never going to love me back.

THIRTY-FOUR

Luke

The house is dark and quiet when I come back from the gym. I gently drop my gym bag to the floor before I head straight up the stairs to Emma's bedroom. She hasn't slept in there since the first night I moved her to my bed, but I have no doubt she's not in my room. Not after what I said to her. And I can't even blame her because I wouldn't want to be near me either.

I pause at her door, my hand lingering over the handle. I hate the idea of waking her up, but I don't want to leave this until morning. I feel like the longer this goes, the worse it'll be and the harder to fix.

Pushing past the ball of nerves in my gut, I open Emma's door. The room is mostly dark, but her curtain is open letting enough light in for me to see that her bed is empty. Hope blossoms in my chest, and I glance down the hall toward my room. Maybe I didn't fuck this up as bad as I thought I did.

I quickly make my way to my room and open the door. Disappointment hits me hard at the sight of my empty bed, and my shoulders sag before confusion makes it way in.

Where the hell could she be?

Maybe she called Bernie?

I go back to her room and don't even try to be quiet now that I know she's not here. The lights illuminate the room with the flick of a switch, nearly blinding me at first before my eyes adjust and I finally get a good look at Emma's room.

What I see makes dread sink further in my gut.

Most of Emma's stuff is gone. Not just gone like she packed some clothes and went to stay with a friend, but gone like she's not planning to come back.

My body drops heavily onto her bed, her faint scent surrounding me and making me feel hollow. What have I done?

My head drops into my hands, my heart aching in my chest more than it ever has. I'm not the guy who falls apart, but losing Emma is a blow I wasn't prepared for. How did I let everything get so twisted up? Why did I lose my shit on her?

Our fight runs on repeat in my head until I nearly break from the weight of the pain I remember in her eyes. I did that to her.

How could I have done that to her? Said those things to her?

I pull my phone from my pants pocket and send her a quick text asking where she is. I need to apologize, but I don't want to do it via text. That doesn't feel like enough after our fight.

I go to my room, strip off my clothes, and take a quick shower. When I get out, there's still no response from Emma. I lie on my bed, waiting for the text message chime to go off. My eyelids get droopy, and before I know it, I'm fast asleep.

My phone ringing wakes me. I sit up with a jolt, briefly squinting against the morning sun, and then instantly check to see if it's Emma calling me.

It's not Emma, but it is her mom. Why is Mrs. Delaney calling me?

"Hello?"

"Luke, honey, I know there's probably a good reason you're not here with Emma and that you're probably busy with football stuff, but I figured you'd want to know that Drew made it out of surgery, and it looks like he should be okay."

Here with Emma? Drew was in surgery? What? My heart plummets, and fear and dread swirl like a tornado in my gut.

She continues, completely unaware I'm about to lose my damn mind. "He still hasn't woken up yet and there's..."—she pauses, her voice catching—"there's a chance he could be paralyzed, but they won't be sure until he's awake and they can run some tests. I just thought you should know since you two boys are so close."

I find my voice, but it still comes out hoarse and confused. "What happened to Drew? Where's Emma?"

Surprise fills her voice. "You don't know? I thought for sure Emma would've told you before she left."

"She didn't." Because I wasn't here, and I'd been a giant fucking ass to her.

"Oh. Drew was in an accident." She fills me in on what happened, his surgery, his current condition, and I hear her words as if I'm standing in a tunnel, the words whooshing through my ears while my heart feels like it's being actively ripped from my chest.

I cut her off before she finishes with, "Which hospital?" I could assume it's the one she works at, but if he was in an accident, they would've taken him to whichever hospital was closest.

"Virginia Mason."

"I'll be there as soon as I can." Before I hang up, I add, "Oh, and Mrs. Delaney, could you not mention to Drew or Emma that I'm on my way."

She sounds confused but ultimately agrees. The second I hang up the phone, I pull up flights on my phone and buy the soonest flight to Seattle. I throw together some clothes and then drive to the airport, breaking multiple traffic laws but not caring. I have to get to my best friend.

But more importantly, I have to get to Emma. I have to tell her I love her and hope to God it's not too late.

I arrive at the hospital right after visitor hours end. There was a delay with my flight, and it took all fucking day to get here. I swear I'm about ready to crawl out of my skin with how desperate I am to see them both.

The nurse takes pity on me and lets me through to see him—especially after I promise to get some signed Wolves' gear for her eleven-year-old son. She points to Drew's door, and I push it open, freezing in the doorway at the sight of my best friend battered and broken.

His head turns from the TV to the door, a look of surprise flashing across his face. "Luke?"

I walk farther into the room, letting the door close softly behind me. "Hey."

Drew's face quickly morphs from surprised to guarded. "What are you doing here?"

I grip the back of my neck. The easy answer would be because my best friend was in an accident, but the truth is I'm here more for Emma than I am for him.

"I'm here because the people I love the most are here."

We stare at each other, both of us too stubborn to look away. I have more to prove here than he does, so I have no intention of breaking first. He needs to know I'm not backing down.

His lips quirk up in the hint of a smile, his eyes slightly crinkled, then he turns back to the TV and points to the screen, where a game between the Dolphins and the Patriots is playing. "Shouldn't you be getting ready for a game?"

"No, we played yesterday and lost to the Seahawks, which I'm sure you'll be happy to hear since that's your team. I have practice, but I called my coach. I won't be starting next game since I'm missing practice, but it's just one game. It's more important that I'm here."

He looks back again and then gestures to the chair by his bed. I take a seat and lean back, pretending my body isn't strung tight waiting for him to rip me a new one about Emma like he did over the phone. Instead, we just watch the game, neither of us saying a word. I'm only partially paying attention to the game. Mostly, I'm trying to figure out what I need to say to convince him that what I feel for Emma is different than any woman I've ever dated before.

"This is the first time you've been back to Seattle that wasn't for a game in years."

He's right. I only come to Seattle when I have to, mainly so I can continue to avoid my asshole dad.

"Like I said before, I needed to come."

He watches me closely, his gaze more hawk-like than I've ever seen, and I imagine this is the lawyer who questions people in court trying to catch them in a lie. "Because the people you love the most are here, that's what you said."

"Yeah."

"And those people would be who exactly?"

I sit up, bracing my elbows on my knees, my hands clasped together. Ignoring his question for the moment, I get down to the heart of it. "I'm sorry, Drew. More than you could ever know. I should've told you when it started. I...I didn't think you'd understand, and based on your reaction, you didn't. So I guess I know you well enough to know I was right, but I still should've told you as soon as I realized where things were going. It's different with her. I'm different with her."

"You love her." It's not a question.

"I do."

"Does she know?"

"No."

"What happened between you two?"

"She didn't tell you?"

"I asked, but she shut down." His gaze turns stormy, the protective brother coming out. "She's heartbroken, so I'm going to ask again, what the hell happened?"

I rub my hands over my face, the weight on my chest nearly unbearable as Emma's face during our fight flashes through my mind. "I freaked out on her when you called me and chewed me out. I was already in a piss-poor mood before you called, but then I lost it. I took my anger out on her by saying some things I never should've said. Things I don't even believe. Then I didn't dispute her when she said I only thought she was casual and convenient for me. Even though that's not even close to being true. I hurt her badly, and I don't know how to fix it."

"But that's why you came? To fix it?"

I meet his stare with my own, hoping he can see how serious I am. "Yeah. I have to fix it. I need her, Drew. I love her. I love her so much more than I ever thought I could love anyone. I hope I'll get your blessing, but if not, then I'm still going to pursue her and do everything in my power to fix things with her."

"You'd still pursue her, even if I said no?"

I give him a smirk that doesn't meet my eyes. "I'd hope you'd change your mind someday."

Realizing he hasn't yelled at me once the whole time I've been here, I ask, "Are you still mad?"

He exhales a heavy sigh before he says, "Yes and no. I'm still pissed you didn't tell me early on, but almost dying tends to put things in perspective. I'll admit, I overreacted. It felt so important to me that you weren't interested in her because you were *my* friend. But you're also the best guy I know. I love you both. I want you both to be happy. I just never in a million years thought you two would be happy together, even though Emma's had a crush on you for as long as I can remember. I really didn't think you'd ever see her that way. I think what really threw me was that I always thought you saw her like a sister."

"I've never seen her like a sister. I was protective of her because you were and because she needed people in her corner. But then she showed up on my doorstep looking nothing like I remembered, and something shifted between us."

He frowns at me. "So it's just about how she looks?"

I shoot him a glare. "You really think I'd sacrifice a lifelong friendship just because of how a woman looks? Wow, thanks."

He holds his hands up in a pleading gesture. "Sorry, man, but that's what it sounded like."

I shake my head before dropping it in my hands. "I can't explain it. I had always found her interesting and unique, but it's like I didn't really see her until she showed up at my house. Maybe it was all the years where our paths didn't cross, or maybe it's how focused I was on getting into the NFL before, I don't know. But I was drawn to her the minute I saw her again."

I look at him, my eyes pleading for him to understand my struggle. "I fought it, Drew. You have to believe me. I fought it with everything I had because I couldn't lose you. But I couldn't fight anymore. I love her, everything about her, and I won't apologize for that, but I am sorry I wasn't the one to tell you and that I waited so damn long."

He stares at me, his eyes darting back and forth between mine searching for something. I just bared my soul, so I don't know what else I have left to prove to him that I love her.

Finally, his expression shifts, and I immediately recognize the sadness in his eyes. "I don't know if you can fix this, Luke. I've never seen her like that. She's more closed off than ever. She wouldn't even open up to me, and I'm usually the one person she'll talk to about anything."

My heart falls—if it's possible for it to fall any harder than it did when I realized she was gone.

He clears his throat. "But I won't stand in your way. If you really love her like you say you do, then I trust you with her. If she'll give you another chance, then you have my blessing."

She has to give me a chance. Because if there's anything I've realized since the moment I returned to my empty house, it's that I can't live without her.

THIRTY-FIVE

Emma

The elevator ride up to Drew's hospital floor feels like it takes an eternity. I hardly slept a wink last night, my mind reliving the moment my mom called me about Drew's accident, over and over again. The few reprieves I got were filled with memories of Luke yelling at me and calling me stupid.

And God, how stupid I was.

The more time I've had to think about it, the more I've realized he was never going to be mine. Not permanently. If it wasn't Drew, it would've been something else. He's a famous football player who can have any woman he wants.

Why would he want me—the woman who's lost her music and her identity in one fell swoop?

Pain lances through my heart—my poor heart that only days ago had me convinced I'd never been happier—and I lose my breath for a moment, the burn of tears behind my eyes. But I'm not alone, so I take a quiet, shuddering breath and suck it up. I have to be strong in front of Drew and my parents.

I especially cannot break in front of my parents. The looks of pity would tip me right over the edge with my already fragile current state.

The elevator doors open, and my parents and I step out, all of us eager to see Drew again. His doctor looks up from a conversation with a nurse down the hall and makes his way toward my parents. I push forward toward Drew's room while they walk and talk behind me. I overhear bits of their conversation but stay focused on the door at the end of the hall where my brother is.

"...Should be able to go home tomorrow afternoon. He's recovering well, and has passed all our checks, but we'd still like to keep him for one more day of observation. The physical therapist will call once he's discharged and schedule his first appointment in the next few days. I've referred him to Haley Rogers, the new PT from New York, who's highly regarded."

"I'm surprised you're going to release him so quickly," I overhear my dad say.

"I would've recommended an extra day, but his disposition improved drastically once his friend arrived."

"His friend?" my dad asks at the same time I push Drew's door open and freeze at the threshold, my disbelieving gaze landing on the one man I should've expected but was not at all prepared for. The blood drains from my face, and I glance down at the floor before his eyes have a chance to land on mine. Oh, look at these fascinating flecks of gray in the speckled floor. Yep, this is definitely a better thing to look at.

"Luke!" my mom exclaims and gently pushes me out of the way so she can run forward and wrap him up in a tight hug.

I will not cry. I will not cry.

"Oh, honey, thank you for being here. It's a relief to know you'll always be here when Drew needs you."

My mom can't possibly know how her words slice through me, but they're just another reminder that he's here for my brother.

Of course he is.

He left me at his house alone but immediately jumped on a flight for my brother. I shouldn't be surprised—it's what I expected all along.

We were never anything serious.

Maybe if I keep telling myself that, I'll finally believe it—or more like my heart will finally give up on this ridiculous hold that Luke has over it.

Deciding I need to focus on why we're all here, I walk over to my brother, my focus homing in on him. He's the only person that matters.

"Hey, how are you feeling?"

"Hey, Squish. I feel like I was hit by a car."

My caring expression immediately morphs into a frown. "That's not funny."

The smirk disappears from his face. "I'm sorry. I was just trying to lighten the mood." He glances at Luke and then back to me. "In all honesty, I'm still really sore, and my ribs ache like a bitch, but they keep me pretty medicated, so I'm feeling better than yesterday."

"Dr. Reynolds thinks you'll be able to go home tomorrow," my mom tells him.

Drew's face lights up. "Really? Damn, that'd be great. I'd much rather sleep in my own bed."

"Luke, how long are you staying?" my dad asks. I don't look up at him, my gaze dropping to Drew's blankets, but my ears perk up waiting for his response.

"I've worked it out with my coach to be here for a few days before I have to go back to LA."

"Are you staying with Drew too?"

My whole body locks up, my hand inadvertently squeezing Drew's. I can't stay in the same place as Luke. Not right now. Everything is still too raw, my emotions all over the place.

Drew's hand gently squeezes mine, causing me to glance up

at him. He watches me closely for a moment before turning his attention to my parents. "Actually, he's going to stay at a hotel nearby since Emma's already taking over the guest room and I didn't want him to have to sleep on the couch."

"Oh, that's a good idea," my mom says behind me. "I'm surprised you're not staying with either of your parents. Your dad just got that new place that's not too far from Drew. It's quite a gorgeous estate."

"Mom," Drew scolds, "I've already told you that Luke doesn't talk to his dad anymore."

I quickly glance at my mom to see her frown at Drew but look properly chagrined. I attempt to look back at Drew, but the pull is too strong, and my gaze is drawn to the man who broke my heart not even forty-eight hours ago.

Has it really been less than two days?

God, it feels like so much longer.

My gaze slides up over the navy blue T-shirt that hugs his chest and biceps but hangs loose over what I know to be washboard abs. Abs I've tasted with my tongue. My wandering eyes drink in the sight of Luke, my body humming with memories of his lips, hands, and cock, while my heart flutters with so much love you'd think there was an entire butterfly habitat in my chest. My green gaze is just about to work its way up to his face when my brain catches up and reminds me he doesn't want me.

The pain that barrels into me at the reminder nearly knocks me to my knees, but I lock my emotions down and force my eyes to look at my brother instead of the one man who will never be mine.

My brother stares at me, his expression unreadable, while the sensation of being watched is strong. I can practically feel Luke's penetrating gaze burning a hole in the side of my head, but I refuse to look his way.

Why does he care anyway? He and my brother seem to be good, so he's essentially getting out of this with a clean break.

He hasn't lost anything. He still has his best friend. And he made it clear what he thought of me, so I don't know what else he could possibly want from me.

If he thinks for one minute that I'll go back to being what was apparently just fuck buddies, he's delusional. If he just wanted a fuck buddy, he shouldn't have blurred the lines the way he did.

You know what? It doesn't matter. He's only here for a few days. I'm stronger than this. I can do this.

What's a little heartbreak?

"How's it feel to be home?" I ask Drew once I get him settled in his bed. He turns on the TV to a sitcom we used to watch as kids and shoots me a smile.

"It feels much better than being in that damn hospital for another night."

I smile back. "I bet."

He lets his smile fade, his serious gaze telling me he's switching topics. "Are you ready to talk about it?"

"Nope," I say, popping the P, and immediately turn around and head toward the kitchen. "I'll make us some dinner."

"I ordered takeout!" he shouts after me.

I don't respond, not wanting him to have any excuse to call me back in there and spill all my secrets. I managed to avoid having to talk about my problems the whole time he was in the hospital because my parents were always around. They never seemed to pick up on the tension swirling between Drew, Luke, and me, and for that I'm eternally grateful.

I drop my elbows to the counter of his kitchen island and

bury my hands in my hair, letting out a groan. I know I won't be able to hold him off for much longer, especially now that I'm living here.

A knock on the door pulls me out of my head, and I move over to my purse on the entry table by the door, digging for some cash for the meal. I'm still digging around in my purse when I open the door without glancing up.

"How much do I owe you?" I ask, trying to balance my purse on my knee and dig around. I really need a better system. Like an actual wallet instead of just shoving my cash in here and cards in the pocket.

"I'd be happy with a conversation."

I know that voice. My head pops up, my eyes wide and my mouth parted in surprise.

"Luke," I breathe out his name and swallow hard. "Uh, I was expecting it to be takeout. Drew said he ordered out."

Luke holds up two white plastic bags. "He texted me, and I picked us up some Thai from that place you love by your parents' house."

Since when does he know my favorite Thai restaurant? It must've been Drew's recommendation.

I stare at him, still completely surprised that he's here.

"Can I come in?" he asks, his lips quirking up in a small smile and his eyes alight with amusement.

Fuck, I'm being a spaz. Moving away from the opening, I pull the door open the rest of the way and gesture inside. "Sorry, yeah. Come on in. Drew's in his room if you want to go hang out with him."

Luke's brows furrow, and his mouth is now turned down in a frown. He glances down the hall toward Drew's room but stays in the entry hallway.

He turns back to me. "I was actually hoping we could talk."

Shit. Shitty shit shit.

What's a girl gotta do to get at least a few days to be heart-broken before having to face the guy who did the breaking? Do I really have to be subjected to this awkward conversation now?

I decide to just get down to it and let him off the hook. Let bygones be bygones and all that bullshit which will be a total lie. Whatever. I don't plan to see Luke ever again if I can help it.

Pulling my shoulders back, I lock down my emotions as best I can and tell Luke what he needs to hear. "There's nothing to talk about. Really, Luke. It's fine. I'm just glad you and Drew were able to work things out. I know that relationship is impor-tant to you. I'm glad our stupid mistake didn't ruin that." I inter-nally wince at the use of stupid, instantly reminded that he called me that during our fight.

Expecting him to be grateful, I'm surprised to see his frown has deepened and his eyes look...sad? That can't be right. What does he have to be sad about?

"Emma..."

No. I'm not doing this any longer. I'm already too close to breaking as it is. "There's no need to drag this out, Luke. It's completely unnecessary. Let's just move on and forget it ever happened."

Needing to escape before my emotions slip past the metaphorical mask I'm wearing, I turn and head toward the guest room, immediately closing and locking the door behind me.

I curl up on the bed and finally let the tears free.

THIRTY-SIX

Luke

That was not what I expected at all.

I stare, dumbfounded and heartbroken as Emma scurries down the hall into the guest room. The sound of the lock reverberates down the hall, making me feel like she's locking me out in more ways than one.

Emma's never been so emotionally shut down before. She's fire and passion, her emotions always showing everything she's feeling in vibrant display. That's not the woman who just made me feel like I was two feet tall. Like I'd just lost everything I never knew I wanted before I had her. No, the woman who just stood in this hall with me was cold, distant, her expression unreadable. That wasn't *my* Emma.

Not knowing what else to do, I make my way to Drew's room where I find him sitting on his bed in sweats and a Seahawks shirt. Normally I'd give him shit about wearing a different team when he's supposed to be my best friend, but I don't have the energy.

I've never felt so lost before.

On the field, I always know what to do, what's expected of me. I live for the cheers of the fans and supporting my teammates so we can get the win. With women, I've never faltered, always knowing the right things to say and do. Well, until Emma showed up.

"You okay?"

I glance up at my best friend, who's staring at me with concern and understanding. Shrugging, I move toward his bed, dropping the food at his hip before sitting in the chair on the other side of his bed.

"She blew you off, didn't she?"

I lean forward, resting my elbows on my knees, and stare at my hands clasped together. "I don't know who that was out there, but it sure as shit wasn't my Emma."

"*Your* Emma?"

I glance up to see his eyebrows practically shoot up to his hairline before he appraises me more carefully.

"You really do love her, don't you?"

Frustration seeps from my pores. "I already told you that! What? You thought I was bullshitting you? I wouldn't do that when it comes to Em."

Drew holds his hands up in a surrendering gesture. "Okay, chill, man. I got it. I heard you when you said it at the hospital, but it's different seeing this side of you. I've never seen you this broken up about a woman, not even Anna."

"Because I haven't felt this way before."

It feels so easy to be honest with Drew about my feelings now. Why couldn't I do this with Emma? Hell, why couldn't I do this with him a month ago?

"I've always held myself back from women, never fully letting go with them because I wasn't sure they could be trusted." I scrub my hand over my head. "But with Emma, there was none of that. Once I was with her, I was hooked. I was more invested than I'd ever been before. And yet, I still never told her how I really felt."

I hate that she still thinks she was just a convenient fling when that couldn't be further from the truth.

"I need to tell her the truth. She needs to know how I feel." I push myself up to standing, the urge to get to her as soon as possible vibrating throughout my body.

"She won't hear you."

I pause and glance back at him. "What do you mean?"

His expression is sad and guilty. "I, uh, I may have said some things when she told me about you two. Things I knew would hurt, but that I thought she needed to hear. I didn't think you could possibly be serious about her."

"What did you say?" I'm angry, but I'm more desperate to fix this, and anger won't get me anywhere.

He closes his eyes and pinches his nose. "I can't remember everything, because my concussion still has my brain a little scrambled, but I remember saying something about how you would've told me if you felt anything for her."

I drop down to sit on the edge of his bed, defeat coating every inch of my body. "Fucking hell, man."

"I'm sorry. I was angry and in a weird, asshole way trying to protect my sister from having her heart broken by my best friend. Although, I realize now I didn't handle any of that the right way either."

"It seems like none of us did." Running my fingers through my hair, I confess, "She wanted to tell you early on, but I told her I needed to be the one to do it."

"But you didn't."

"No, I didn't." I huff out a humorless laugh. "Because I'm a fucking coward."

Admitting it is painful, but it's the truth. I was a coward, and now I need to fight like hell to win back the one woman who's ever made me believe in love.

THIRTY-SEVEN

Emma

My grumbling and gurgling stomach wakes me up, reminding me that I never ate dinner last night because I was trying to avoid Luke and then fell asleep waiting for him to leave.

I roll out of bed, and not bothering with my appearance, make my way out to the living room and kitchen. The view of Seattle from the large floor-to-ceiling windows pulls my attention away from food.

This might be my favorite part of Drew's apartment in lower Queen Anne. His windows and balcony have the perfect view of the Space Needle, the Puget Sound, and Mount Rainier in the distance. It feels serene in the hectic, bustling environment of Seattle.

"Morning," my brother's gruff voice startles me, and I spin around.

"What are you doing up? You should be in bed, resting." I rush over to him and grab him carefully under his elbow to help him.

"Em, I'm okay. My head feels a lot clearer today, and I was going stir-crazy just sitting in that bed. I thought I'd sit out here and eat breakfast on the couch and then go back to bed after."

"Fine, but let me make you breakfast. You just sit on the couch."

He rolls his eyes but doesn't fight me, and I don't miss how out of breath he is when we get to the couch. Yeah, he definitely underestimated the extent of his injuries and limitations. I go into the kitchen and get a pot of coffee brewing before turning to the fridge and getting all the fixings for cheesy scrambled eggs with ham. I nibble on a banana while the pan is heating up so that my stomach can chill out with all the grumbling.

My brother's voice infiltrates through the sounds of the coffee brewing. "I've let you put this off long enough. I need you to tell me what happened with Luke."

Without turning around, I answer, "Didn't he tell you?"

Luke and my brother seem to be back to normal, so obviously Luke told him everything.

"He told me his side. I want to hear yours." There's no anger or malice in his tone, which is a relief. At least he's willing to actually listen this time instead of just get mad, not that it really matters now though.

I shrug, still avoiding eye contact and focusing on our breakfast. "Not much to tell. You were right." I'm proud of myself for how steady my voice sounds, even though I'm dying a little inside the more this conversation goes on.

He's silent for a minute, and I start to think maybe it's going to be that simple and he'll drop it now. But I should know better.

"I was right about what exactly?"

Oh God, is he actually going to make me say it? Closing my eyes and taking a fortifying breath, I respond, "It wasn't serious for him."

"He said that?" His tone says he doubts Luke would say that.

"Not in so many words."

"Emma." Oh, great. He's got his lawyer voice on. Lovely. "Look at me."

Reluctantly, I turn around. "What?" Okay, maybe that came out a little more like a bratty little sister than I intended. Oh well.

"He said it wasn't serious for him?"

"Drew, I really don't—"

"Answer the question, Em."

"No, he didn't say that exactly. I said that I was just convenient for him, and he didn't disagree." I drop my gaze to the island counter, fighting back my emotions because I'm so sick of crying over Luke fucking Carter.

"Em," my brother starts softly, but I speak up before he can say anything more.

"Don't patronize me, Drew. I get it, okay. You were right. I was the naïve girl who got to finally hook up with her lifelong crush, but it didn't mean anything to him. So can we just move on? Clearly you two are back to normal, so let's all just forget this ever happened and call it a day, shall we?"

"No."

My mouth parts slightly, my eyes widening fractionally, but it's like my brain can't quite process his response.

"What the hell do you mean, *no*?"

"We can't go back to normal. I don't think anyone wants that, least of all you."

"Um...correct me if I'm wrong, but weren't you the one so pissed at the idea of us together that you told me I was delusional and then hung up on me?"

"That was before."

"Before what?" I'm so confused about what's happening right now.

"Before my accident. Before Luke told me the truth. Before I really processed everything."

What did Luke tell him?

No, no, it doesn't matter.

"If you know the truth, then why won't you let this go?"

He stares at me, and for a second it looks like he's amused with me. I swear to God, if my brother hadn't just been in an accident, I would sucker punch him in the gut right now.

"Because you clearly don't know the truth."

I shake my head in dismay. "I don't understand where you get off telling me I don't understand the truth about my own relationship, or lack thereof."

"You need to talk to Luke."

My heart pounds erratically in my chest. "Why? So he can tell me what I already know? Trust me, he made things abundantly clear. I get it."

"You don't." He says it so sure. Like if I just listen to Luke then the world will be all sunshine and roses. Maybe for him, but that's not how things work out for me.

I shake my head, the sting of tears coming on faster than I can control. "Stop," I plead, my voice breaking.

Drew's face falls. "Em—"

I hold up my hand, stopping him. "Don't, okay? Don't say this shit and get my hopes up when you and I both know Luke and I were never meant to be a thing. I'll get over it." Not likely, but he doesn't need to know that. I hid my crush from him for years. I'll find a way to hide my heartbreak too. "Please, I'm begging you, just let this go. You get to have your best friend all to yourself. I'll stay out of it from here on out. He's all yours."

I turn around to find the oil is burnt, so I take the pan to the sink to clean it before I start all over. Although, the idea of food now sounds about as appealing as ripping my toenails off.

"Emma." Drew's voice is soft, like he's afraid if he speaks too loud, I'll dash out of here. He's not wrong.

"I'm not trying to get your hopes up or cause you more pain.

I'm trying to help. You know I'd never purposefully put you in harm's way. I love you. I love Luke too. And he's hurting a lot. You really need to talk to him. I promise I won't stand in the way anymore. I give you guys my blessing."

I spin around, my tears now coursing down my cheeks and anger burning like fire through my veins. "You give your fucking blessing?"

Drew's eyes widen in surprise at the derision in my tone.

"Your fucking blessing for what, Drew? Luke and I are nothing. *Nothing*," I spit out. "It was a mistake. One I'll never make again. Let it go."

My body is urging me to throw the pan in the sink and storm out of here, but I need to take care of Drew, and I won't skirt my responsibilities no matter how much he's pissing me off.

Drew's face gets stormy, and he closes his eyes and takes a noticeable breath before speaking again, his patience with me clearly running thin. "Stop being stubborn and listen to me for one second. *Luke is hurting too.* You think he'd be upset over someone who meant nothing? You think he'd risk our friendship for someone who meant *nothing*?" he says, adding air quotes at the end.

Some of my temper fades as his words start sliding through the cracks in my defenses.

"I love you, Squish, but sometimes you can be so damn stubborn that you get in your own way. I know part of this is my fault because the things I said when you told me were hurtful. And part is definitely Luke's because he was a dumbass, but you've got to give him a chance to fix it."

"If you're saying all this because you're worried things will be awkward, you don't need to worry. I won't make things awkward."

He frowns. "I'm not saying this because of me at all. I'm trying to get you to give Luke a chance to talk to you. I can see how miserable you are, and I hate it, especially since I know it's partly my fault. But Emma, you have to believe me when I tell you you're not the only one who's heartbroken."

His penetrating gaze pleads with me to believe him, to hear him.

Luke can't possibly be heartbroken because that implies I meant something to him, and if that were true he would've corrected me during our fight.

Right?

THIRTY-EIGHT

Luke

My fist pounds on the door, my body aching to be near her. The minute she texted me that she wanted to talk, I rushed over here as fast as I could. This is my opening, and I suspect it's the only one she's going to give me.

This is my chance, and I'm not throwing it away.

Emma opens the door, and relief floods me at the sight of her. Her gorgeous green eyes are wary, but I'll take that over the distance she gave me when I was here last night.

"Hey." I sound breathless, but I can't help it. God, I miss her. Even though I saw her yesterday, I've now gone four nights without sleeping with her body curled into mine, and I'm damn near desperate to have her in my arms again. To be able to touch her and kiss her and show her what she means to me.

"Hey," she says, her face starting to get closed off.

"Don't do that," I plead.

Her gaze snaps to mine. "Do what?"

"Emotionally shut down. I can't stand it. I need to see all your emotions, Emma. I need to know how you're really feeling."

She watches me cautiously for a beat before she nibbles the inside of her lip and gives me a brief nod of her head.

Thank fuck. One hurdle down. Now I just need to convince her to give me another chance.

She steps out of the way and gestures for me to come in, which I do without delay. "Where's Drew?" I ask.

"He's in his room watching TV. He said he was turning up the volume so he can't eavesdrop." She rolls her eyes, and her lips tilt up into a small smile. We both know that nosy fucker is definitely going to be doing his best to listen in.

"Do you want anything to drink?" Emma asks, fidgeting with her fingers. The nervous gesture calms some of my own nerves.

"No, I'm good."

She nods and chews on her lip before her gaze lands on the couch, and she moves to go sit down. I follow her, and when she sits on one end, I fight every urge in my body that tells me to sit right next to her and instead sit at the other end. I know her well enough to know if I crowd her, she won't hear me.

And I need her to hear me.

"Thanks for inviting me over."

"Drew said I should hear you out." She nibbles her lip again, and the movement draws my gaze straight to her lips, noticing for the first time that they lack her signature red color. Instead, they're her natural pink—the color I've only seen when I've kissed off her lipstick.

"He said you were hurting," she continues. My eyes move up her face to observe the disbelief and hesitancy in her gaze.

"I am," I tell her honestly. There's no point in being too proud to share my feelings now.

A confused expression crosses her face when she says, "I don't understand why. You and Drew worked everything out. You guys are fine. He's not mad at you anymore."

My chest feels like it's caving in that she thinks I'm only concerned about Drew. Did she feel that way the whole time we were together? I think back on our mostly perfect month and a half as a couple and try to see my actions from her perspective.

"You always thought my priority was my friendship with Drew."

She looks at me like it's obvious. "Well, yeah."

Fuck. I messed this up long before I ever realized I messed it up. And I realize now that by not telling Drew from the very beginning, I just reaffirmed her belief that Drew was my priority, even though that wasn't my intention.

"Drew is important, but he isn't my priority. At least, he hasn't been for quite some time." I scoot across the couch, needing to be closer to her. "Emma, you're my priority, and it's been that way since I first kissed you."

I'm no longer surprised by the shock that streaks across her face, but it does gut me in a way I'm not prepared for.

"I hate myself for making you ever question your value in my life." Unable to hold back any longer, I reach out and hold her hand. She doesn't pull away, which I take as another small win. "You are irreplaceable. You are everything I've ever wanted that I never knew I needed. My fear over telling Drew wasn't ever really about Drew. It was about how I could keep you. That was always the driving factor behind my hesitancy to tell him. I didn't want to lose you."

Her eyes fill with tears, one finally slipping free down her beautiful, freckled face. I raise my hand to brush it away with my thumb. Her eyes fall closed in a look of pain and relief at the contact. I know the feeling.

"Emma," I whisper, getting choked up myself. Her eyelids slowly lift, and the openness in them nearly does me in. "I'm so sorry, Em. More than you'll ever know. I'm sorry I ever made you doubt my feelings for you. I'm sorry I didn't tell Drew the minute we got together, so I could shout it from the rooftop like I wanted to. I'm sorry you thought I would choose him over you. I'm sorry I let you walk away that night thinking you were just convenient. But most of all, I'm sorry I never told you the truth."

"What's the truth?" she says, her voice soft and hoarse.

Letting my thumb graze across her cheek, my gaze locks on hers as I say the words I've never said to another woman. The words I mean with every cell in my body. "I love you."

She launches her body at me, her arms wrapping around my neck. I catch her instantly, pulling her as close to me as I can, letting her legs straddle my hips. Our lips crash together, longing, need, and love in every touch and caress of our tongues.

She pulls back just enough to look in my eyes. "You really love me?"

"I really do. More than words could ever fully describe."

"I love you too," she says softly. I don't think I've ever heard more wonderful words.

"I want you back, Em. I want you in my house, in my bed. You belong with me. In LA where you can pursue your dream."

Her shoulders sag. "I can't. My music is gone."

I tilt her chin up until she looks at me. "It's gone for now, but you're too talented to give up. It'll come back. I believe in you. Come home with me." I kiss her, hoping I can seduce her into agreeing because I can't live without her, and at this point I'll do just about anything to get her to come back home.

She breaks our kiss, resting her forehead against mine. "I can't. I promised Drew I'd stay here and take care of him until he gets back on his feet. The doctor said he can't be on his own."

"Good thing I already arranged an in-home nurse then, isn't it?" We both turn our bodies to look at Drew, leaning against the door—probably to actually hold his broken ass up—watching us with a smile on his face. "By the way, Squish, the nurse will be arriving tonight, so I'm gonna need you to get your stuff packed up."

Emma bursts into laughter, and I swear on my life, I've never heard a sexier sound. "You planned this?"

He smiles like the cat that ate the canary. "Oh, I hoped for it."

"What were you going to do if I said no?"

"Kick your ass out for breaking my best friend's heart."

She rolls her eyes dramatically before turning back to me and planting a loud kiss on my lips. She pulls away long before I'm ready to let go and gets off my lap, heading toward the guest room.

"Where are you going?" I ask.

She glances back at me. "To pack."

"Does that mean you're coming home with me?" I can't hide the hope in my voice.

"You're sure you want me to?"

"More than I've ever been sure of anything."

Her smile lights up her face, but it's the heat in her emerald-green eyes that has my cock pulsing in my pants. She disappears into the guest room, and I turn to Drew who has a smug grin on his face.

"I knew you two kids could work it out."

I shake my head at him. "Yeah, okay, Mr. She-won't-hear-you."

"Okay, so I might've had some small doubts, but I'm much more naturally optimistic than you are."

"Whatever. I'm just glad she's giving me another chance."

"As you should be. This is the time where I'm going to stop being your best friend for a minute and talk to you as Emma's brother."

"Okaaayyy." I arch my brow at him, curious where he's going with this.

He tries to straighten up, but ends up leaning back against the frame, his face paling a little bit.

"How about you scold me while I help you lie back down."

He nods. "That's a good idea."

I wrap my arm around his waist and let him lean on me as I help him walk back to the bed, his breathing labored, no doubt from his broken ribs.

"Ribs bothering you?"

"Oh, you know, just every time I take a breath, but no big deal."

Laughing, I respond, "But clearly it hasn't killed your sense of humor."

He sobers a bit. "Like I said, almost dying changes your perspective on things."

Once I help him get settled back in bed, he pins me with a serious stare. "Okay, pretend we aren't best friends for a minute."

I fight a smirk. "Okay."

"If you break my sister's heart, I'll hunt you down and break every bone in your body and spill all your secrets to the tabloids."

"And what will you do if she breaks my heart?"

He cracks a smile. "I'll bring you a six-pack and then be your wingman."

I shake my head. "Let's hope it doesn't come to that."

Drew tilts his head. "Wait, are you telling me you're already planning the wedding with my sister?"

"Well, seeing as how the past three days were some of the worst of my life and I'd like to avoid that at all costs—not to mention the fact I basically just invited your sister to move in with me—I'd say marrying her down the road isn't a stretch."

Drew just stares at me before he breaks out into a huge grin. "Holy shit, you know what I just realized?"

"What?"

"If you marry my sister, then you'll be my actual brother. What the hell are you waiting for?"

We both burst out laughing, which of course causes Drew to groan in pain from the strain on his ribs.

Emma pops her head into the room. "What's going on in here?"

Drew and I exchange a glance before I look at Emma, soaking in her beauty and her presence. "Oh, you know, just guy stuff."

"Uh-huh." She doesn't buy it, but she doesn't question it. We order out for lunch and hang around the apartment until the nurse comes to replace Emma. By the time we head back to my hotel, my body is on fire. All day long, Emma has given me light and gentle touches that have turned me on in immeasurable ways.

Time to return the favor.

Emma walks through my hotel room door, and I follow closely, grabbing her hand and spinning her the second we both pass the threshold. The door shuts at the same time I push her up against the wall and take her mouth in an owning kiss.

One that tells her very clearly that she owns every piece of me.

She moans into my mouth, our tongues dueling for dominance, while her hands slide under my shirt, her fingernails scraping against my skin.

My fingers weave through the silky strands of her red hair until I have a solid grip and can hold her in place while I devour her mouth.

It's been too long since I tasted her.

My lips work their way down her neck, tasting every inch of her I can, needing to sate my craving for her. She tilts her head back and arches her body closer to mine. My fingers slide under the hem of her shirt and pull it slowly up her delectable body, revealing her creamy white skin one inch at a time.

Her lust-filled eyes watch my every move as she bites her luscious lip between her teeth. I pull her shirt over her head and toss it to the side before taking her mouth again, kissing her hard.

My cock strains against the zipper of my jeans. I want to take my time with her, make love to her, but I'm so desperate for her, I don't know how long I'm going to last.

Without a word, her hand rubs over the outside of my pants against my painfully hard cock, causing a groan to release from my throat.

I need her naked. Right. Fucking. Now.

I pull her pants down her legs, dropping down to my knees so I can kiss her thighs. I want to get lost between these gorgeous legs of hers. I slide my fingers slowly up the inside of her legs until I reach the wet apex of her thighs. I slide them easily through her slick lower lips before pushing one inside. I pull out and push back in, adding a second finger, then a third. My gaze watches her face carefully as her eyes close in bliss at my intimate touch.

With a groan, I bury my face in between her thighs, tasting her musk and flicking her clit with my tongue while I pump my fingers steadily inside her. Her fingers tangle in my hair, pulling almost painfully, but it's such a welcome pain after so many days without her touch that I don't complain.

"Luke..." Her voice is breathy as she fights against the orgasm. "I want you inside me."

I don't stop my ministrations to answer her, determined to make her come this way first. She'll get what she wants because

I want nothing more than to be buried to the hilt inside her, but not until I'm done tasting her release.

She grips the back of my head, holding me in place as she loses control of her body and grinds her convulsing pussy against my face. She practically suffocates me with how tight she's holding me against her.

But damn, what a way to go.

Her legs shake as her release washes through her, and her body sags against the wall once her orgasm has finished. I lick her once more before making my way up her body, taking a nipple into my mouth, then the other, until I finally reach her lips in a brief kiss.

While she catches her breath, I shove my pants down and kick them aside, then pull my shirt off by the neck. Once I'm naked, I pick her up, her legs immediately wrapping around my hips. I push my cock into her, and we both groan in pleasure at being connected like this again.

No one—and I mean, absolutely fucking no one—has ever felt this good.

I fuck Emma hard against the wall, giving her every piece of my heart with each thrust. When we finally both fall over the edge, we hold on to each other tight, letting our releases wash over us until we're completely wrung out.

I kiss her neck and then pull away enough to look at her. She has a pleased smile on her face, her cheeks flushed, and in this moment, I'm determined to keep that look on her face for the rest of her life. I want all her orgasms, all her love. I want to be the father to her children. I want to be her everything.

Never again will I deny what is so painfully obvious to me now after almost losing her. Emma Delaney is the love of my damn life.

THIRTY-NINE

Emma

8 months later

Nerves flutter in my belly as the lights hit the stage. I take a breath and close my eyes, soaking in the sounds of the room—shuffling feet, the clink of drink glasses being set on tables, the low murmur of people talking. I slide my fingers over my guitar, the feeling of being fully joined with my instrument one I'll never take for granted after what it's taken for me to get here.

Luke and I flew back to LA the day after we got back together. He had to get back to team commitments, and I needed to get back into therapy. I continued seeing Jane twice a week, and after a month, I finally heard the soft whisper of a song in my head for the first time in nearly two months—the longest I've ever gone without my music.

It's been seven months since I first got my music back, and I've been playing almost nonstop, writing songs about my experiences since I moved to LA—the fear, the hurt, the love. Two weeks ago, I took the plunge and signed up for this open mic night. When I told Luke about it that night at dinner, he insisted on telling all our friends, so the crowd is filled with friendly and supportive faces. Bernie, Drew with his physical therapist turned girlfriend, a bunch of Luke's teammates along with their significant others—Gabe, Will and Gina, Jack and Paige, and Matt and Nikki.

Most surprising, though, is the fact my parents are in the crowd. They've never once shown up to one of my performances, but they came out just for this. Our relationship has come a long way since Drew's accident. My mom and I talk once a week, and very rarely does she criticize my life. It might help that she thinks the sun rises and sets on Luke. Insert eye roll, please.

Although, I can't really blame her. He's easily the best thing that's ever happened to me. His unwavering support these past eight months, especially after particularly brutal therapy sessions, has been a godsend. Some days I even pinch myself because I still can't quite believe that he's mine.

Pulling my thoughts away from the man who has captured my heart, I caress the strings of my guitar before strumming the first chord. Writing this song became therapeutic and healing in its own right. It was the first song I completed after what I'm now referring to as my music hiatus. As my voice carries across the bar, everything fades away but the words, the melody, the feel of my smooth guitar strings under my callused fingers.

Nothing exists in this moment except me and my guitar.

I hit the last chord and let the music fall away on its own, my eyes looking around the bar but barely making out any of the people due to the brightness of the lights shining in my face. Silence permeates the space in the final second that the music fades away before the roar of applause hits my ears and a smile breaks across my face.

I did it. This was my test for myself to see if I was ready to pursue this crazy career again, and I passed. I can do this.

I walk down the stairs from the stage and straight into the

waiting arms at the bottom. Luke's arms wrap around me as he nuzzles against my ear.

"You fucking rocked that, Em. I'm so damn proud of you."

I pull back enough to press my lips against his in a kiss that's far too chaste for my liking, but our friends are already circling us, so I end it quickly and accept the numerous hugs from our group.

It's not until I get to the group of Luke's teammates that I notice an extra person I wasn't expecting.

"Trent?"

"Hey, Emma. That sounded incredible."

A blush breaks across my face. "Thank you." I mean, what else do you say to the man who's had two platinum albums and a documentary with a popular streaming service when he tells you that you sound amazing?

Luke wraps his arm around my waist. "I told you she was the real deal."

Trent shoots me an amused smile and points at Luke. "You have quite the cheerleader, I hope you know. He all but insisted I be here."

I smack Luke's chest. "I'm so sorry, Trent. I'm sure you had a million other important things to do."

"Don't apologize. This was worth it." He rubs the scruff on his face. "Actually, I have a proposition for you."

Curious, I respond, "What's that?"

"Well, one of our openers for our upcoming tour just dropped out—a family issue—and we have an opening. You interested?"

My jaw drops, and I think I might even black out for a minute.

"Are you serious right now?"

He nods. "As a heart attack."

I swear I try to keep my cool. Really, I do. But how do you keep your cool when all your dreams are finally coming true?

So instead of playing it chill, I jump up and wrap my arms around Trent's neck, squeezing him in a tight hug as I squeal "yes" over and over. I quickly let go once my head catches up to my body and step back, feeling Luke's rumbling laughter as his chest presses against my back and his arms wrap around me from behind. Trent says something about texting me with more details later before he walks over and joins Will, but I barely hear him, distracted by the man behind me and the adrenaline coursing through my veins at the realization that I'm really making it happen.

Luke kisses my neck before turning his mouth just enough to whisper in my ear, "Better not be doing any of that hugging business on the road, Em. I don't share."

Goosebumps tingle down my spine in the best way. "So same rules we use for your away games apply."

He growls low in his throat and my panties are instantly soaked. Not gonna lie, I love him like this. "They definitely apply. No one else gets to have me but you, and vice versa."

Spinning around, I wrap my arms around his neck and finally kiss him the way I wanted to when he greeted me as I got off the stage. I kiss him with all the love in my heart.

"I love you, Luke Carter."

He pulls away just enough to look me in the eyes. "Do you love me enough to marry me?"

"What?" I whisper, barely breathing.

"I thought I could wait, but I can't. I love you, Emma. I want you to be my wife. I was going to do something big and romantic, but I don't know what's more special than proposing after you've just had the night of your life."

"Yes," I whisper, so quietly in the loud bar that it's clear he doesn't hear me when he continues.

"Unless you want something big and romantic, which in that case, pretend I never asked. I don't even have the ring on me."

My face lights up. "You have a ring?"

He nods. "I got it when I was in Seattle. It was my grandmother's. I figured since you love vintage, you'd want a vintage ring, and my grandparents had a marriage for the ages, so that's gotta be good luck, right?"

"Yes!" I squeal, launching myself around his body, my legs tight around his hips and my arms wrapped around his neck.

"Wait. Yes? Like yes, you'll marry me?"

I laugh, happier than I ever remember being. "Of course I'll marry you."

After all, I've spent my whole life wanting to marry him.

I've always belonged to Luke Carter, and now I finally get to call him my husband.

Thank you so much for reading Taking the Handoff! Curious about Trent? Noble Intent is available now!

Gabe Romero's story, Defending the Backfield, is up next!

AFTERWORD

Whew! Where to begin with this one? This was a tough book to write for a lot of different reasons. The biggest one was that Emma is the first character I've written who's the most like me (not everything about her, but we have A LOT of similarities and some of her anecdotes may have been true stories from my own life). I thought writing a character so much like me would be easy, but it was not. It required a vulnerability that I sometimes really struggled with. And then those voices in my head spoke up: what if people don't like Emma? Then they probably wouldn't like me. It spiraled from there. It's was easy to write her reactions because I just thought about what I might do, but it was so hard to open her up and spill what she was really feeling on the page. Her insecurities, her heartache, her embarrassment and frustration over being so emotional. All of that required me to relive my own past experiences and pull out those feelings that I've lived with. It was hard. But it was also rewarding and in some ways cathartic. So, if you don't like Emma, don't tell me LOL.

Despite the challenges that this book presented, I'm really

happy with how it turned out and so thankful to all the people who helped me make it happen.

To my squad who talked me off the cliff every time these two drove me crazy.

To my best friend, Rikki, who's brutal honesty helped me fix some pretty glaring issues.

To my incredible editors at Happily Editing Anns. I'm so grateful to have found you.

To my amazing cover designer, Kate Farlow, who always makes the most beautiful covers for my books.

To my family for your never ending support, especially when I'm up against tight deadlines and need to hide away in my office to get everything done.

And to you, reader, for supporting me on this crazy amazing journey and helping me make my dreams come true. I couldn't do any of this without you.

ABOUT THE AUTHOR

Cadence Keys writes steamy contemporary romance novels full of heart, heat, and HEAs. She loves football (especially seeing all those tight ends), coffee (it sustains her), and watching Gilmore Girl marathons (witty banter for the win). When she's not busy writing, she's spending time with her family or getting lost in a good book (always romance).

You can also find more information about all future releases at www.cadencekeysauthor.com/

ALSO BY CADENCE KEYS

LA Wolves Series

In the Grasp

Across the Middle

Down by Contact

Taking the Handoff

Defending the Backfield

Rapturous Intent Rockstar Series

Noble Intent

Forbidden Intent

Devoted Intent

Promised Intent

www.ingramcontent.com/pod-product-compliance
Lightning Source LLC
Chambersburg PA
CBHW050838190726
48286CB00007B/2133